Breaking the Soul of a Folk

by

Shirley and Jonathan Burey

PITTSBURGH, PENNSYLVANIA 15222

RoseDog Books
701 Smithfield Street
Pittsburgh, PA 15222
Visit our website at *www.rosedogbookstore.com*

ISBN: 978-1-4349-3153-5
eISBN: 978-1-4349-7220-0

Leaders the Almighty heard the cries of unrest let's hope it hit THE Soul of wit.

To avoid scenes shown in "The Grapes of Wrath" over stand that Equality is the righteous path.

HOPE

By

Jonhathan Burey

Hope is the word that first comes to mine for those who have none.
Hope may seem like a four letter word for those who are born with a sliver spoon in their mouth.
For you see Hope is the companion of those waiting aimlessly for virtue in their lives because it is the idea for better days.
So, if one does not have HOPE then they are just living a life on repeat having nothing to be complete.

Breaking the Soul of A Folk

Table of Contents

In search Of My Soul

Table Of Contents

The Forethought

As W.E.B.DuBios wrote so eloquently affirms in his collection of essay written in 1903 that it's beneath the dignity of a human being to beg for those rights that belong inherently to all mankind.

And from the writing of the most influential leaders labeled the father of the civil rights movement in America Mr. Booker T. Washington who wrote in 1867 that we must design strategies that allows accommodations to advance all people regardless of their economical condition. Because Homeless people dissevered to be treated with dignity and respect with decent food and are afforded privileges of important computerized or in a vocational aspect not made to be given chores that make them to feel like modern day slaves. They are entitled to be able to earn wages decent enough for their family to keep and maintain there home once given the proper means.

The present system of leaders must over stand that the world in a circle as my granny would say. Hey now listen to me child and in this big circle one must be ready for a change because it's not flat so one must be ready to not just roll with the flow.

But to move with the punches then one can be in this world for everything not anything. You see, my child anything comes fast and quick it's what those street people want they are out there for anyone or anything that come in their lives and will do dam near all that is put into their face like be with woman or men of ill intent.

But daughter you must be in this world for everything that takes time and planning to accomplish one must slowly studies there mistakes and never forget that once one let the devil ways into their lives it hard getting it out. Never allow anyone to remove one from the arms of the Lord because many think that they do not have to answer for where there life on earth been and committ much sin without repenting nor faith but child the older one becomes the closer they're to those pearly gates.

Yes, so all one has is their soul to keep it wholesomely whole sins are test of our brotherhood on earth so child never carry hate. Because as long as you learn something before reaching deep into hell's gate that no one fate.

Of The Soul of America

O hears and sees the plight of the Homeless fight to save their soul.
They come with dirty faces to stay in heartless places enforced
Using policies on spoken intent to keep aged procedures of wicket
Consent but they will rise in common voices -standing strong against
Policies that do not bring dignity of their human right that places them
All on Devilish plight.

Of The Leaders of Progress

In our Leaders we must proclaim those that are free of prejudging.
We must assure that once chose that they will stand firm and stay
Strong by the choices in the External House.
For Angels are sending out remaining immortal and pure.
Who sentimental and do not weaken the folk.
Using its tender soul to rise to the top leaving a
Legacy that can not be brought nor stopped.

(From soul of black folk, Jung Frau Von Orleans, IVI

As The Homeless Melt

Although I am Homeless but happily, O my mother and father of Jerusalem,
As the people of faith, on the streets of Babylon in the arms we lay.
Cast down upon my sins for he that hath let he throw the first stone.
For now we are Homeless but not helpless lacking hope.
Because the darkness has been my only friend and caused from my own.
Having us to be in spaces of ill guided policies that places us in the vineyards
Of unempathic being using unrealistic means to try to control my every dream,
Enforced by procedures that goes to the extreme.
So for always I have prayed to know my limit in what every I do and I'll
Keep praying deeply to the Gods above to restore in these nations shelters
Dignity and Love.

A Song of Solomon

Cures

Chapter 1

Here in lie words when read shows the passion of human sorrows. Between me and these words I ask an unasked question in which I ask with the up most compassion from one tax payer to another, when did being Homeless become a crime.

It's like the world shutting one out for being Black. Having to be subject to ridicule searches and outrages of human treatment that makes one blood to be boiling inside.

And yet being Homeless is a strange experience- peculiar even for one who has never been on the out side of the spectrum. A people thus down ought not to be asked to feel corrupt with the world, but rather allowed to give some of their time and thought to its own social contribution to society's problems.

In the dark shadows of despair the very the very soul of the homeless soils. While the sociologists restfully count then as bastards and crack heads, as the homeless are caught into a web of ignorance. As if their despair has placed prejudice against their very soul. Causing a striving of their Spiritual being making them the homeless against the criminals. To which the homeless cries out to almighty God and present leaders to do away with the modem day procedures that causes our children to be placed in constant sorrow believing there no tomorrow. Allowing discouragement to settle in their soul's becoming vastly unholy.

Is this not the Star Of Hope in which suppose to be established to give all citizens some type of hope so they can cope in a world that's so very unevenly divided among the haves and the have not. Are they all wrong or all false-you see I feel that each one alone has or had one simple dream or even imagine a world where we all was given from birth a simple thing such as a home. But in true all their thoughts are melted and welded away once arriving in shelter like the Salvation Army in Miami, Detroit, Santa Monica and Houston in particular the Star of Hope missionary shelters. Where they along with there children are reduced to the lowest of human being not even being allowed to watch the news on neither television nor use of anything that's not provided like pure vinegar to help control the many bugs that craw daily. To be really true the training such as the placed like the Goodwill industries that were located on Jensen Street in Houston should be back into place for the needed using up to date technology.

Having training schools so very badly needed today more than ever. They can provide training for the deft, the quick eyed crack heads, the broader (foreigner), people who depend on others for their care, and pure minded clear hearted people. This merely gives an underlying of principles of the great battle of the Homeless problem. In which test the good humor of us tax payer and the sorrowful souls of homeless cries to be placed back into society filling whole which restores their selfworth

Because as we allow the souls of our folks to be broken we weaken the entire flock of people, on their own personal pursuit to find happiest.

Now we as a people should try to live by the Native American ideology written into their ten commandments. For they had to fight in wars to save there people and lands of previous generations. They long ago realized the world's circle therefore they knew that they could not stop the revolving of life's changes.

So as one nation of people who fought in war over lands that we do not properly care for shall remember as we kill off generations of people from the U.S as well as in the Middle East we must never forget that the earth is our mother and we must treat it as such and care for her.

Having us to honor all of our relations and stop taking for granted that she'll always be here for us decades to come.

We should forever give our heart and stop breaking the souls so we all can give to the great spiritual being.

Respecting all life treating each one as they are sacred, and humans.

Take only what we needed from the earth and nothing more than we need to live in peace and harmony on earth.

We must start doing what is needed to be done for the good and safety of all.

Always's give constant thanks to the great spiritual Gods for each new day and never take it for granted that the earth is ours.

Try to speak positively the truth but only of the good in others and never dwell on the bad of others or the negative aspect of their personality.

Understand the rhythmus of nature and retire with the sun awakening with the sunrise. Above all else enjoy life's journey, but leave no tracks.

CURES

The winds are blowing causing the beauty to be shaped
like, a diamond shining in the SUN.

The heart of my preaching is that GOD give me true
LOVE, to invest in all people.

To spread love, God gave daddy the power to love.

Daddy have the heart, and Grandpa died in a great war for me and our family to give hope caused they did not have any.

The stars are beautifully shaped like diamonds.

The trees are beautiful. So help those that have NONE…

Colors of People
Chapter 2

There lays a problem in the Twentieth-first century the Homeless-line there relation to be broaden as an island of problems. As the phase of this matter which is an underlying cause of wars in this nations as well as the Middle Eastern world. From north to south the unfixed technical points of racism to terrorism and local mainstream is caught. Nevertheless, as we know the question of the Homeless is through-out the nation, because no sooner than Israel's armies touch soils of wanted terriortories of Lebanon the question came about-what shall be done with the homeless?

It is the aim of this essay to bring to the forefront of the minds of the world the underline SOLUTION to the biggest problem we face in this here century.

In order for our nation to move-the old, women, and children who with frightened eyes whimpers from starving in darkness of shelters of lost hope.

Two solutions of dealing with this matter are simply using logical means instead of useless schemes.

Unlock the barriers which cause the flood of homelessness and clearly decide what must be done with the Homeless arriving daily into shelters around the world, Particularly this country. We must now establish a Homeless Bureau unlike any present day HUD low income housing which will cut the red tape and give people some assistance in purchasing small acres of land which was stated in the 1927 fair Housing Act.

A bill shall be introduced into Congress and the president must sign into LAW giving a new department of housing along with non profit organizations such as adult assistance training programs to establish modern regulations for keeping and the purchase of housing with the proper training facilities.

To really help the homeless lease them lands, adjust their wages and have them appear in civil court as their counter partner for any fraudulent claims.

Place limitations attached to their grants and organization to make permanent placements. To stop the revolving doors of the thousand of homeless people who are back into shelters within two or three months of them finding housing.

The Bureau can use all abandon properties to be placed under this department of housing for eventual lease and sale to homeless people in acres along with training on actual jobs like Goodwill industries does with the handicap in places like Detroit Michigan and Houston used to do on Jensen Street.

Thus, the United States government was founded on the basic that two or three united can accomplish more than one whom stands alone. For Know man is an island. We must all act as if we're the family of our homeless to decease the number of homeless people in our country forever. Let's this be our legacy to our children for decades to come instead of corporate greed this plants a deadly seed.

Street Soldiers

A Street Soldier is one who lives in the hood and willing to ride for the thing that they believing and always try to achieve. Because the youths of today are very quick to pop a cap and hold onto their ground but a true street solider never fools around.

They will seldom back down nor pretend that they are hard and not cry like a baby after catching a felony charge.

For they always know that their reaction brings consequences of being locked up. So they remain on a whole other level of thought and are never bought. They do not follow those gangsters star rappers who only talk about their baling because those are the ones who are always falling.

For a real street soldier may have not attended college but they get lots of street knowledge. So when one sees their peers acting all bad street soldiers tend to become a little mad. Now, if you see youths that write on wall or folders one understands right then and there that they do not know what it takes to be a street soldier.

FREE READING

COLORS OF PEOPLE

What a world we live in that only sees the color of peoples skin, in order to let one in.

Now, all of us must realize that the colors of people, should not matter as we climb the ladder. Nor in establishing what one's like inside their mind, body or soul.

"Cause just looking at the colors of people, one could never see the true beauty that resides within all God's creatures...Never...never allow people to be stereotyped according to one's color, which does not enable people to be viewed by their action.

To only judge people from the reactions of there race, is such a waste...Surely we could learn something about one's individual personality before we treat them with less formality. So, try hard people of today, never merely see one's color without first looking at people as people. Giving everyone the same amount of respect that all would enjoy.

All should remember that in the struggle for equality and justice we must see the person, not their color rather their WILL.

NO MAN STANDS ALONE

The Days of the ungodly souls are soon to be gone. The wrath of the wicked man will only be left standing for the decades to come. So righteous people, do not be feared for these are the times that test our faith in each other.

Now we must walk with pride and do not hide nor be afraid because these are simply, the last of the wicked man ways.

The Burden
Chapter 3

This new department of housing can give some type of poetic justice by establishing homeless people the rights to forfeited lands of high costing landlords.

Giving tax amnesty to property owner along with commercial breaks to who rent to own or provide actual training which leads to a job paying enough wages to keep their home. In which can be only passed down to their next generation to come or reentered in the Bureau for sale and/or leased.

Nevertheless, several things will be accomplished we will end the cycle of repeated homelessness and cut down the amount of physical suffering so we all do not fall\into a Sea of Destruction. And transport thousand of homeless children from the congestion of shelters in place like Miami, Ft. Laderdale. Los Angeles, Detroit, and Houston. Lastly we will no longer icesolate the homeless from the entire world and bring them with their children back into the mainstream of our society. Which will surely stop the breeding of terrorist youths whom are flooding our cities thought-out this nation?

However the success of the Homeless Bureau lay in the planting of free training among citizens who are of a workable age that posse or can obtain a high school diploma or a general educational degree and/or equivalent.

The opposition to the Homeless Bureau maybe that there will be people who are only out for fraudulent schemes and somewhat bitter. But the Federal government can have investigators working under the Bureau to freely examine any matters that the Homeless or governmental body know are set up for fraudulent purposes. Also, there maybe some bitterness toward this agency but in the end we all as human being of this generation can benefit because if nothing at all we would be slowly and effectively be doing a way the menial system of housing where people are put on waiting list for years and sometimes they die before ever obtaining a home. And the tax payers will benefit because they'll no longer be paying for shelters that does not solve the problem but work with the Bureau acting as a referral branch to do a way with simply providing a short term solution to a life long problem. This will end the cycle of lost hope and ignorance that most feel towards the homeless population today, making them fill less like criminal more like law abiding citizen who like in a system of tax payer who really and truly care. Because they over stand the needs of the common man. This will give their children and our elderly a sense of actual hope instead a filling they fallen down a harsh slope. Causing them to never want to stay striving at the bottom of the rail but feeling that our American tax payer understands their private HELL. To bring all that want the power to feel independent again to rear their children to become productive warm loving individuals who learned from us old to bring in this world their children wholesomely as their life unfolds.

As in the writings of one of the influential founding fathers of their time who was the author of a book written at the brink of the civil war named Thomas Paine.

He wrote a book called "Common Sense" and there are some words that I'll never forget in about 18th century which are so right for our present times. He states that as long as we live in a society that affords one individual to be born into a world inheritrently advanced and another to be born without even the proper means to obtain at least a home. Then we as nations of civilized people will continue to fail. For myself I truly have seen a land that was much like an Utopia where the river were clear. Having the sunrise to where people of all races traveled on highways and were beholden to only God's commands.<**> duties and deeds to be performed -the problem with the twentieth-first century is the problem of the Homeless. For they place a burden on all of our souls we must help them to be whole for they shape our future.

A Sea of Destruction

THE BURDEN

Hey listen, don't y'all hear the beating of the drums.

They are becoming louder with every generation, displaying acts of violence.

Having the drums to continue to beat harder, passing the torch to the oppression of decades to come.

For equality will run the world like a river stream. In each generation the drums beating will get stronger, until your law becomes a fair reflection on the oppressed, for he will come clean up the rich man's mess.

Yes, equality will come too for certain to all God's creatures. Then and only, the oppressed will no longer be carrying the burden, for GOD will close the final curtain.

A SEA OF DESTRUCTION

Oh Lords of all moral men the world is wondering. Will there be any more peace.

And harmony among people of various religious faith. In the name of what God will they keep destroying this land with their bear hands.

For many are also wondering will this be the cause of destroying our earth while they fight to decide who came first.

What history will we teach our young as we become a society that ruled by a bullet or bombs. But many fail to see that power is to be used to control.

However, "Absolute Power" posses a firm hold.

Therefore; leaders must stop and listen to all parties concerned so we all do not blow up and burn. For love and wisdom will pull us through no matter what our leader decides to do. Making the way for kindness and forgiving to shine on through. So leaders must walk in the path of a prudent man and start legislating laws for the oppress so we all do not fall under in this mess.

Yes, these are the means that will enable us to become free.

To simply live. Then our soul will be saved from being taken back to their caveman days.

Tell Them
Chapter 4

From the pits of sorrow; without words us tax payers must assure that all funds being allotted to the Homeless are used in the proper manner. So the children of this generation can be given hope for brighter days. If not they will continue to run wild in the street like beast in human form killing anyone in vain remaining untamed. Also, one never knows when they will be Homeless themselves that why we must strike the blow to let everyone know that our country affords all to grow.

In our history we have had some very influential leaders having some to stand out.

An overwhelming one was Mr. Booker T. Washington, using his ideas these words I'll bring to the forefront as he stated in 1800's. He felt then as I do now that we must pass the days of astonishing commercial development and use our sense of doubt.

Let's stop overlooking the Homeless youths who are born into poverty by just the luck of the draw and by know fought of their own.

Mr. Washington brought into our minds a simple definite program at a moment when our nation was on the brink of destruction much like today. Having our lives on the war in the Middle East not centering upon our youths. As he wrote we must concentrate our dollars on educational training. We should strive more to build computerized and industrial schools, and trades that fits today's needs. You see we must stop treating the Homeless like criminal as they do in many shelter such as the star of Hope and build an alliance with the best of the Homeless in order to linked them back into the masses. This will bring about enthusiastic, people of a strong faith with an unlimited amount of energy into programs that will change their present path of life instead of simply drug testing to control their way of life.

Tell Them Now

NOW!
TELL THEM

> In order for this nation to be based on Integrity, honesty and equality they must over stand that our leader is only a common man, and they must carry the plight of fighting for their natural rights. Yes, they brought drugs to confuse the oppressed, but somehow God Showed the power to invest. Using modernism to be there test, of faith in helping their fellowman, when it does not put them out on a limb. For the elite will pay for treating the oppressed this way. Just tell them to keep a clear mind and listen to the elderly, for they will lead them to eternal life, for they have gotten old and paid the price. Then you will be moved into a earth, that no longer will be carrying the deadly curse.

To gain empathy we must cooperate using several of elements comprising the Homeless with institutes or compromises and we must demand a complete surrendering of political equality; among conservatives, using generously conceived working trends of a mutual understanding of the plight of the needs of the Homeless nation wide.

Causing material prosperity to all that seeks not neglected Home that seems to aim of obscurities or despair.

Then we must stop the narrowing of neighborhoods that singling out their visions of glamour making them envious of people of elitism. For it is easier to do ill than well in the world and to criticize the Homeless. But designing educational programs that allow one to express their spiritual being within this world and acknowledging ideas of self sacrificing of endeavors of worth. To give them training to obtain wages will empower them to bring their youths out of the dark conveners of thought.

Placing interest and opinions that will retain their respect of all. Mr. Booker T. Washington

1867

Now, there among the Homeless are educated and thoughtful minded people.

Who are sincere and honest and endeavors are worth of purpose ordinary indeed.

As American citizens we as a people must demand an end to all prejudices against each culture.

And call for a complete overview of the present housing system. So, we can stop enacting programs that tend to have the Homeless submit to policies and procedures that is clearly inhumane.

History shows of nearly all Homeless people a doctrine of self-respect is worth more than lands and houses. Also, people who surrender voluntarily their attitude about the world definitely is worth saving.

We must stop the thinking that Homeless people will only survive with a hand out not with an opportunity to achieve as they need.

This way of thinking causes them to give up their three most important aspects of life that's critical to their survival which are political power, civil rights, and higher education and training of the Homeless youths.

FREED

YES, THEIR SELF ESSTEEM WAS HELD DOWN. Being sold as cattle but somehow still fought the battle. And pray one day at a time that tomorrow would be forgiving then kind never ever will there be a time again that the slavery of a people will settle inn. You see, Equality is not only for the betterment for the Africans-Americans but it reflects the hopes of all citizens by every means necessary.

Malcolm X

NO MERCY

The Almighty will have NO MERCY on the souls that are the cause of destroying of Innocent lives. For we all will have to individually come to those Pearly Gates. No matter what's one religious faith.

Yes, even the meek and sheik will have to answer to THEE. For equality will be the mean of the righteous rulers, and the Almighty gives

Know preference to any particular religion or race. So, we all must have clear clean hearts and stay brave, for kindness and forgiving

Will be the only traditions that are saved.

FREEDOM
PEACE ON EARTH

Peace on earth is no curse. The curse is on the earth that all people should have peace and liberty to become free. Now, why can't you see that God will not let go until peace is released.

A World of Cry's
Chapter 5

Nevertheless nothing effectual has made the Homeless programs seem more hopeless than recent change in direction of our missionary shelters. The vast numbers of shelter located in several of states like Texas, California Michigan and Florida has down right declared war on the whole Homeless population. Places such as Detroit has made their Homeless people go through so much red tape many just sleep on the streets.

And in Los Angeles or Santa Monica their Homeless people have to get on a waiting list. But in Miami and Ft. Lauderdale their Homeless population is sent on a type of merry go round being sent to shelter after another simply told to go to police station and call 911. After calling they make you wait for hours saying someone will come to assist you but they never come or when they do they simply send one back to sleep in the shelter's parking lot along with your children. It happen to my 11 year old son and I we were send one place by a worker at the Miami Salvation Army that was not even open any longer. Having to go to the Ft. Lauderdale library and finding one once getting there we were told by the attendant to go to the police station. Once arriving at the station an officer told us to go back to the shelter at 942 7th street and stay in the parking lot and don't leave till morning. While at the shelter's parking lot several of people were there and another attendant wouldn't let us use the restroom and kept asking us to leave all night. Once day light came we found on our own way in Ft. Lauderdale when asked if we wanted to go back to Houston we said yes. I can only feel sad for the children because I wanted to teach in the lower income areas because I felt if I could get my son to read on a 12th grade level while he was in the 5th grade then I could teach other.

After returning to Houston we were out of money because the church only gave us a hundred dollar gas card therefore we had to spend all of our funds on hotels.

Now in Houston we were placed in a room after we slept on a hard cold floor with nothing to eat for over ten hours waiting for an intake worker. Because of my lack of planning we were subject to some of the harsh treatment and rules along with poorly prepared meal and subject to sereaches that were clearly in violation of our 5th and 6th amendments of the Constitutional rights. The present policy in the Houston shelter treats its guest as if they have broken a law of simply being Homeless having them along with their children to stand without talking against the wall while receiving meals that smell bad taste worst that one would not prepare for an animal. They along with their children can be put out for violating any or none of the shelter's rule. Also, there is a good thing that the Dowling Street shelter is that they do provide, mother's with their basic personal needs. For themselves and their infants, unlike the other states mention that do not give a dam unless one is a user and or abuser.

Because the shelters in Miami are so full the case worker's mind is on over load meaning. That they just can't here another sad story one can see this in their eyes.

But whom one should feel empathic for is the children who are by no fought of their own are force to live a life without TV, computers and several of things that youths need to become a law abiding citizen in this present day society? And who are tease at schools making them just simply wanting to drop out. Having to ride van clearly label. Also, attending schools that don't properly keep accurate records of where there at while on school grounds. Before my son was taken out of the Denstatnated School offered by the shelter when I went to pick him up the shelter nor the school official's knew what class nor where my son was for several hours. The workers at these places look upon the Homeless population as simply being a burden upon society and it's there fought that they didn't pay there rent. Never truly having that unbreakable belief that some Homeless are tax payer and fell into a saturation that all they need is a little time to get back on their feet. Like in our case I really left to re-united my son and dad and the underlying reason was my present landlord who waited until summer vacation to raise my rent after I refused to resign the lease because I wanted to buy a home that could be left after I'm gone. And I worked all my life being in my late forty I felt if I could just leave him a home then half of his life's battle would be won.

Now one must ask our nation of civilized people is this the legacy that our generation wants to leave for the next. Having them not even to be granted any civil equality while on earth nor while they are homeless.

Today the attitude towards the homeless is not as one would assume, in all cases they are not crack heads, drunken who constantly have to subject to drug test. The same ignorance was placed upon many people of color and they rise. Hater of the homeless fail to see that they may also be on the other side one day.

Therefore, we must not allow anyone to label all of them as menace. Simply people who came in-to some bad luck after making some wrongful choices.

And stop allowing shelters to reduce or in danger them into becoming modern day slave locked inside of a room where insects crawls into their bed, no food, and at least let them bring into there living space something non toxic such as vinegar an old time cure use to help control bugs where they sleep.

This is my cry's to the world to restore in our shelters meaningful chores and in our schools modernized trade which allows our youths to no longer be afraid.

They can enter our world with a decent trade. While in shelters like jail cell with the surrounding of discontent if the policies of these places were to help them rather than just collecting money they are in a position to remove away their self pity and doubt and give them a decent way out. It is this failure in our present policies that must be ended one that constantly threaten to write up individuals that has shown no cause. Such as in my case when I was threaten being ask to leave because I did not have a job verification form that had the letter head of the company when I told them that my job informed of a knew system which had a phone number using an employment verification code. But they refused to call because someone had a form with my employer they still refused and gave me time to get the form. But why should a shelter take a person through all this just to work in the shelter where they already paid taxes to live until their back on there feet and to be constantly written up. For thing like coming in to later once you have signed out to be out late on a late log is totally uncalled for what do they want a family to do come and sit in a room looking like a jail cell with noting but sleep or read not even having any-thing to eat because one surly cannot eat the food they sever without becoming ill. Also, you have to sign paper to the effects that you won't talk about the place nor comment on anything once you're a guest. Now wait I thought this was an American country where we had freedom of speech this is a clear vio-lation of ones 1st admen-dement.

But at the star of hope missionary shelter one has know rights while they are homeless. Now, if the policy maker does not stop funds to these programs that do not protect individual civil rights we will not have the moral fiber of this country to survive. The legislators' have a duty to perform not send aids to come walk around and see the surface talk to the people stay a few days and then examine the orientation policy. And if they must work provide jobs that are payable because once I saw a woman mopping the floors with her infant child in her arms and her two toddlers sitting across in a chair and old women whom worked all their life having to wash, mop and various of other chores. You see, as I stated before it's good to have them work for their stay but pro-vide some type of training aspect that would give them actual certificate toward real employment that can lead to a real wage paying job.

This would place our society in an upward movement when we provided industrial or techelogical training for the masse number of youths that are forced to be in shelters through-out this country. We could help them to get back on their feet and the youth to strive to aid their parent once reaching of age and Houston who is so very far advanced than any other above mention shelters can sever as a model for the rest of the shelters Located in the United States.

As our forefathers stated this would bring into our world ambious minds that every civilized society must posses to continue to peacefully strive. The convicted criminals even have their civil rights protected and they committed an offense so why by just being HOMELESS THEY DO NOT.

So, we must never ever allow any generation to ever forget these words. "WE HOLD THESE TRUTHS TO BE SEL-EVIDENT; THAT ALL MEN, WOMEN, AND CHILD ARE CREATED EQUAL; THAT THEY ARE ENDOWED BY THEIR CREATOR WITH CERTAIN UNALIEN-ABLE RIGHTS; LEADING TO PROPERTY."

Of The Leaders of Progress

In our Leaders we must proclaim ones that are free of prejudices.
We must choose those standing strong by choices in our external house.
For Angels are send out remaining immortal and pure.
Who's unsentimental that does not weaken our folk.
Having tender souls rising to the top and won't allow
Oppression to weaken the flock.

(Inspired by Jung
Frau Von, Orleans,)

A Substitute's Prayer

Oh Lord of us all I pray that you allow me to remain Humble and not stumble for trickery has gotten very bold which cause us to lose their soul. Causing miseries to the extreme having us not wanting to accomplish our dreams. So, lord of us all please help us to stay cool while traveling from school to school.

A WORLD OF CRYS

Crys for the world for the winds are blowing strong, sending the locust to march on through.

For the elite must stop their greed cause the oppressed will no longer stand for their misdeeds.

Now, deep down in one's soul one has to wonder why does this world have to be so very hard even with a professional job.

For money may bring a lot of materialist dreams and pleasures, but a childs love is forever.

You see, to kill one's fruit of love that was sent from God above is a mortal sin and anyone that does this will never live again.

Yes, yes I cry for the world, not only this girl because children are a gift from God that nurtures ones relationship and to kill them will not give one fame, only shame. I cry for the world for not properly treating this disease.

Now who's the blame? I cry for you too 'cause without ones offspring they miss the love that a child's love brings. Yes, like a warm day in mid-spring the love of a child is so innocent and clean. Just as a hot summer night that brings unconditional love that sanctions from the Heavenly Father above, so is a child's love.

Yes, yes, yes I cry for the world, not only this girl.

TWO SHOULDERS ON GOD

Two shoulders on God, the Angel is on the right side and the devil is on the left which means, it makes one do good or bad. If you have different problems talk to the Angel or the devil...if one talks to the devil, it will get one in lots of trouble.

If one talks to the Angel, it gets rid of all your nightmares, and all things that frighten you, cause talking to the Angel, will get you unconfused.

The devil might say, take his cards because he really likes them. But you must not; and talk to the Angel. The Angel goes and talks to the devil and tells it to stop his devilish ways in confusing the kids. The devil must stop and go away. Then your shoulders will be with only GOD, the Angel on the right, and a God who shows the kids the Angel controls his brain. Then you will not have to strain too much in life.

Two Shoulders on God

Chapter 6

Once in the late 1990's I taught in Los Angeles in schools for troubled youths. At this time the street gangs ran wild numbering into the hundreds. Having most of the youths to not fear the police or their chopper even giving them a street name calling them ghetto birds. But what stayed with me the most is how nothing seemed to bother them like the domed sense of lost that most possessed.

They shared in feeling that their life was going to turn out just as their parents. Because the same opportunities were afforded to them just as their parents and they were just born on the wrong side of the tracks into a world of gang banging and street pharmacy. Having the lack opportunity in every community being the underlying cause for being born into poverty. It was just the luck of the draw to live and die.

They basically lived to expect to die at a very young age some did not think that they wouldn't live past their teens. Anyone came into their hood was on their grounds and must have a pass to move around or they would surely be dealt with most usually carried some type of weapon and were not afraid to use it no matter who was around. This was simply let revealing gangs no whom hood you were in especially if one entered with certain clothing or hair colors.

Yet there was among them a half awakened common consciousness, sprung from common fun and grief at burials and the birth of a child. Also, from common hardships in poverty of the lack of technological training. Realizing that their life was hard because there was not hardly any neither vocational nor computerized training open to them neither in their community nor at their schools that they felt gave them enough in wages. Some youths do not believed they have choices they saw their parents struggle as their own and our public schools most do nothing that actually train.

Being in the same gang that their parent's parents were in just as the some pass down their homes to their children the street gang goes from generation to generation. Most over stood how the veil of opportunity would not be truly afforded to them. Because they lived and went to the same school that their parents and witness while growing up the poor wages, killings and the total shutting out of the corporate world. Once I met a young woman whom most youths were afraid of even the teachers did not want to confront her when she came on campus and was not supposed to be.

After we talked she turned out to be not so fearful at all her street name was Snookie and she was an African American of a slim stature and was very serious. She was actually there that day to protect someone. But they showed respect because she was in a gang that her mother mother's was in and her family have a lot of deaths while in that culture dating back to five generations. As she explained, you see they fear not me but what my gang family can do if they disrespect me because I got generations into gangs starting with my great grand father and mother. She and her mother is the 4th and 5th generations still alive. Also, she said that if she ever had children that they would have no choice but being in a gang if not just for only protection on the streets. A saddest came upon her dark brown face as she said; it's a shame that all we can pass down is our way of life.

Because the world won't change unless you make away out of the jungle and remember that God's the boss but in the hood everyone knows the code And the cost.

Because one must take a chance to make their way out of this stone cold jungle and if that means to be born into a gang to stay feed then in the hood that's like an unwritten code. Then she started leaving saying we over stand that our glory will come in the next world. But for now we got's to get paid like everybody else and protect our back cause it like a jungle out here my click keeps us from going under. As she was in the distant she finished with by the way you got's a free pass to come into the south central click anytime just tell anyone who fuck with you that Skokie got you're back hollered.

Walking away she left a life long impression in my mind because she realized her role in life and was determine to break suddenly it occurred to me that this is what we as a nation must do with the Homeless population. We must allow them and their youths to make a change by taking a chance on training them to make their way out of the shelters throughout this country. Enable for them to see that they are not bound to that type of life. If they are willing to work at a vocational training that can surely pay wages for their family. Withstands their dim view of themselves of lacking self worth. Then their recollection of this world and their childhood are not filled with puzzling outcomes that are acted out in their deviant behaviors. And can change their way of thinking of adult's leaders today. From being less empathic and greed into thinking highly of our communities in general, displaying less hater of programs designed presently for training. Because the shelter's ridicules their parents with written write ups that are belittling. Wanting them to lose their stands built among a mother and child and the schools don't care because they don't even keep records of where each child is saying thing like I hope we do not have an emergency .Once when I came for my son after an hour of trying to located my son while on HISD school grounds they took over an hour to located him They do not allow any happiness while in the shelters maybe because they do not want the homeless people to enjoy there stay. But worker can smoke outside not having to walk two or three blocks wristing their lives with three children or less. They do not have to give any respect once a young worker talked to an older lady so bad that I felt sorry ever complianting about washing. Wishing that I could as another worker said go somewhere else and wash on my own. Tearfully I replied soon I will but as a tax payer whom never ask anyone for much I will wash here.

I so wish because being Homeless meant anyone even a child can treat you or talk to one any kind of way and they can't defense themselves without being threaten with write up and being put out on the streets with your children.

You see the first altercation started over the worker demanding the women who was scheduled to do chores take out wet blankets because she let another guest take my washing period? After another worker gave my time to someone else because I have left clothing alone at the door while I went to wake my son 7am. Now you can't leave your children along so why she could not call cause of policies.

You 'all asked to leave but that's not all parents are written up for being out after curfew when they follow their rules. It's this type of treatment that must be stopped we are not living in a dictatorship because youths are watching the first person that they respected being treated inhumanely having the parent losing control of their children. Hell were homeless not hopeless why can't they have an unbreakable belief that not all people are the same and to break the chain of Homelessness we must stand by the parent until their shown proof of unworthy or disrespect. That most people are basically good inside they have just fallen on poor planning from bad choices and most intent to do the right thing. Just because they have fallen upon trying time they still needs to be treated with dignity and homeless does not allow nor require them to make a total invasion of their entire life show the homeless parent some respect after all most are tax payers and law abiding citizens.

Now, our journey at the several of shelters is painfully in the past. Behind us lay tales of mountainous proportions of problems with policies that are causing the breaking of the souls of a folk. For when reading this book we should ask ourselves in our present circle of progress when it come to the Homeless how shall we measure their ability. Why should we care because as myself until we were Homeless we simply thought of them as crack heads, people who were losers uneducated or simply ones who did not want anything in their lives. Lastly people who dissevered what ever hand that God gave then because of their own poor planning and choices. Remembering when I was young I always said that people lives are guided by the choices they make and the path they take. But as I became older I see that the older one becomes the narrowing of life's choices and the boarding of one ability to lose.

You see as I took a trip form north to south and back again I ask with no pun intent how long shall we treat our youths with such abuse and throw away valuable people like the elderly that worked on this earth years and whom could sever in these shelters as adopted grandmas for the very young. Who will grow into adulthood hating our present programs that are ruled by unempathic workers using wicket means to control their very dreams while they push the Homeless lives to the extreme. We should care because in the word of an old women who carried us all it's not what you been it's threw but how you came out. We all will have storms there simply of the norms so stop placing the Homeless as if there unseige. To stop this nation from falling into a twilight of darkest that keeps us on the brink of some ill fainted downing days of dissenter.

As we lead our Homeless population into a ternary of dictatorship we must stop to think of the children to not lead them astray. Thus, amazinging rode joyfully amusing seeing racism from north to south witnessing much of the Jim Crow law to be still in effect. Let's not enable the Homeless population to only see star's on top while their dead. They also may have two shoulders on God right here on earth.

A Wife's Pain

Laying still remenEiscing of memories of long ago causing a flowing of a past as if it was yesterday.

Entering in one soul of a love that s gone cold. Pearing one heart as if it was hit by a ton of bricks having the pain to run very thick.

Allowing one to become torn leaving only the love from our frist born. As vows were broken a passionate glow arise into ones soul.

Causing a chilling of the flesh that removes one stress.

Now, we must go our sperate ways with only ourselves to blame tarnished by the memories of a wife's pain.

Without Knowledge
Chapter 7

In Homeless shelters the case workers are like a store house preacher embodies the vast number of problems that the homeless faces everyday. Some of the workers are empathic but the majority are burn out of having to deal with so many cases that constantly comes, on to their case file for instance. The shelters in Florida especially Miami, and Ft Lauderdale workers are overwhelmed with the hundred of Homeless mothers.

Having their space to be taken up by the victims of drug abuse and HIV clients.

Once my son and I arrived in Miami-Dade we were given a booklet printed by the mayor office under Carlos Alvarez, the booklet stated that their mission was to provide excellent public service which addressed their community needs. Also, it states their pleased to provide residents with a guide to locate services having an array of them available to all residents wanting to stay in Miami-Dade county.

Now this essay will describe our visit to Miami and its surrounding cities.

Once arriving in Florida my son and I went to Fort Lauderdale to visit his dad after a ten year period. Although he wanted us to come we realized that we could not stay with him because his present condition.

However, my real purpose was to teach because before leaving Houston I called the Miami-Dade County school system and talked to personnel located on BiscayneBoulevard. After talking to someone in the office they assured me that substitute teachers were well needed and even got paid more working in zone areas, in low income neighborhoods. I got on the internet and paid for sixty-one dollars for the background and fingerprinting. But once we arrived we realized that Miami did not want its children to learn because they do not even have a system installed that selects the subs randomly. I was told by a another sub that the principal at each school that you go must like you or you will not be working and there no way of getting a fair jobs placement daily.

The first day we arrived in Miami we rode down Biscayne we wanted to eat driving the opposite way we spotted a McDonald's deciding to turn around and stop to eat.

As I turned the car around I pass the place and turn into a doughnut store next door. As I was coming onto the lot a police car with green and yellow printing was behind me. He told me not to move with his hands moving close to his gun. He immediately said the reason he stopped us was that I make a u-turn as he was following. I said yes but, that's not wrong it's not illegal because I turned into a parking Lott not in the street. He said give your license and proof of insurance and if there was not any warrants he'll let us move on to our designation. Replying I don't and he took my data. While it was being ready to come back, he told me that he stopped us really because it looked like I was trying to hide some drugs because I turned around as he was behind. Drugs I said I do not have any I came here to teach, he then looked at me giving me back my data saying where are you going I said that after we got something to eat that we was looking for a hotel giving me back my data a strong look came upon his beige skin with dark brown eyes saying how much do you have to spend for a motel. I said about 50 or 60 dollars I don't know why. He turned his body around facing what I learn was to be closer to the downtown area always from what called north beach a very upper section of Miami. I said you mean I can not go in the direction that I want I have no warrant you said I was free to go and at this time I saw a young man riding with him who was looked to be about 14 or older wearing a Jew mica which is a small hat worn by the people of the Jewish faith. The officer also looked of that faith because he had very dark hair and then told me that Miami was a straight up and down place with water on both side one way out and one way in so what do you want to do. I said you mean I can not go any farer pass 79th street someone told me to go across 130th street to find the best places. He then got into my face that when I could see a name that looked like Benjamin not seeing his badge number because he tried not to get to close and when I tried to come into closer to him He repeated one out and one way in and besides there is only two motels left across 79th street and there both over seventy dollars a night this is not Houston everything is high here so if you do not want to go to jail for driving erratically you better turn that car around and head that way pointing towards the downtown area.

Just then the young man move his eyes as if to say please just do what he said because he nodded his head as if he was in agreement with the officer so we did and found the owner of the Royal Inn on the same street to be very understanding and let us pay 50 dollars instead of the usual Saturday night price of 70 dollars but as the days turn into a week we ran out of money and we became victims of false advertiment from the hotels that were in the coupon book such as the Holiday Inn express located on LeJune street and Motel 8 in the 3000 block of Biscayne and refused access to the Inn Continental hotel in the downtown section of Miami. The door man put his arms in front of the door blocking us saying that if we did not have a room them we could not come in I said you mean this is a public facility and I can not come in so, I and my 11 years old son could use the restroom. Other people are here to escape some of the heat just sitting; He still refused so I pushed his arms from blocking the way and asked if I could see the manager. A white lady at the desk gave me a card of the person in charge saying it's a shame that you people still have to fight to be treated with respect and I'm sorry you son had to see that man treat yaw that way. But in Florida we quickly found out that most motel have a heart and they caters to prosecution having a city that do not give a dam about the future of it's children nor do they care about saving there souls because in the next chapter I will talk about what happen as we traveled along the still Jim Crow south because it got worst even an adult at Wal-mart something that still haunt my son and I today.

You see all my life I had to fight from the time I came to this world now I'm still fighting this inside racism that not suppose to cut into ones soul but none of them hurts me more than what happen in Metairie Louisiana where I was assaulted by a guest host for going back into the same door. The fights I had with the Publix store over a roast beef sandwich. Miami do not want their children to rise above the poor condition. However the upper part of Florida is not any better when it come to being Black in America.

As they treat their Homeless people worst than any other state that we encountered. The next chapter will describe our very, cold but real treatment in the place we labeled without knowledge because the people are fighting a struggle presently.

And some can not see the battle of economic equality that was started in the 1800's under Presidential administration after the next.

So without knowledge of these aspects our generation is doomed to keep fighting racisms of people that never even known their names.

Because our creator made one race of people and we as a nation of civilized people labeled them the human race.

Let's find that equality is the vehicle to bring us back to a place in this world that affords all that seeks the rights of the Meeks. For the seekers will inherit the earth not who came first.

Because as I grew in balls of fire got worst as the riots of 1967 became thrown in my back yards. Remembering a conversation and an incident of how it was explained to me. The next chapter describes my encounter with the racism of my youth. After leaving school visiting my granny whom explained the whole civil rights struggle in this manner.

WITHOUT KNOWLEDGE

STARS ON TOP

A young man is wondering what's in a star? He wants to know if the stars were like the sun or if the sun was like the stars. He's found out that there was nothing to tell about the stars and the sun. He really found out that he was going to discover a knew thing like a space ship looking like the stars. But, David was too sick to tell all the people.

That it's a comet and something goods is going to happen on earth…like water and fire mixing up the sun and the stars putting them together making us shine like a new moon.

WITHOUT KNOWLEDGE

Without knowledge one never sees when death and destruction will come calling. But many people will never forget feeling those victim's pain and shock as death came early that September 11 morning giving everyone no clear warning.

Yes, for many that was their last day on earth.

So, without knowledge ones life may leave just as the wind blow between the trees with just a blink…

We may one day understand why they had to kill so many women and men in such an evil way. For God will have the final say and beam the unrighteous to a world that's with greed and disease that will take all their seeds.

Yes, Lord of Lords and King of Kings please guide our rulers to do the right things. Because for generations to come our children will never forget all those human beings, shattered dying in the streets. Therefore without knowledge we came and without knowledge we will go.

A Mother's Cry
Chapter 8

Of the training of our people why from the dirt on the side of men coming on earth with a plan fling oneself with pride while aged slowly one sprit subsides.

For one soul's peak as age allows one to become weak mending their mind of the last remember to repent your sins of the past.

While traveling from different frames of thought hoping your sprits are not caught. For the wickedness of greed plants a deadly seed but righteously one succeed. While in shelters of ill fated hope one prays hard to cope.

So in darkness one cry not to fall astray but to surround one self with positivistic.

For naked we'll come to those pearly gate leaving behind the dirt that was implemented to you on earth.

From the marching of the civil rights movement I was born into a world of on fire with racism and greed. With hatred of each other that it seem to be part of the norms but I was determining not to let any of those matters get into my way.

However all that came about on a summer day while attending Duffield elementary. On the playground the year was 1967 and I was in about the 6th grade.

Noise was heard someone shouted they killed him and from that point the street of Detroit Michigan were burning. A teacher had us on the playground whom was white at this time many of my classmates did not talk about race because we all lived in a black area and color was not important to us we were ten but as we played the people got loud. Our world was about to be thrown like never before as the crowd got to the play ground my teacher saw that they began throwing rock shouting they killed him over and over. People were crying and suddenly my teacher was hit on the forehead bleeding he grabbed me and got us off the playground into the school. But I did not understand what was happening and far as I was concern they always killed someone in our neighborhood. But the teachers were being attacked and some got hurt really badly. They explained to us that an important man was gunned down and named Martin Luther King. The police came to help the teacher's get home but we all walked home with our sibling...But we knew that there was going to be trouble most of us did not understand but we were happy to get out early no matter who was killed, thinking as I walked to my Granny's house. Once over there she did not want me to go back out so she ask me to French braid her hair we turned on the television and it was on the news. I asked granny who was this man that they killed and she told me his name was Martin Luther King the man who was our leader and I ask why was the people so mad because they killed him I do not understand they killed lots of people around here why was he so important.

She replied that this man was what the old folk called a freedom fighter. And I said and why do they care about him they liked Malcomon X was he also a freedom fighter.

She said that they both wanted the same thing but one wanted it by any way and the other wanted one to turn the other cheek that meant you should be passive. Also, she told me to remember that freedom anit' free and the price one paid for freedom should not be taken for granted nor you must not never let no one take it away from you because our ancestor fought all their lives to obtain the rights to be treated with dignity no matter what your live saturation was an even if you did not have a home because we all are going to get old and died and that if we as a people do not learn to live together affording all that want a fair chance to advance regardless of their race if not there will forever be fighting and killing each other.

You see, child every generation get greater than the next because nothing and no one can live forever nor will they stay the stone everything will change just like day turn to night. And never judge because God the creator made one race and we labeled it the human race Now, child the world not flat it round rotating constantly changing decades after you see a whole knew world. They can kill all the leaders they want you see equality will come maybe not in our life time but it will. I then asked her what is this thing they fear why do they hate us so granny what did we do. She said listen to me child and never forget that people are living creates that survives in a wild kingdom of animals that fears what they do not understand this is the plight of the common man. If you do not embrace a change then your world will remain the same always be ready for a change because that's worldly progress. So Mr. King had an inside much like he fought for all children who could not fight for themselves in order for people of all races have a fair opportunity in every community. For us to understand that we all can seek to have the beauties on earth. Having our test in brotherhood on earth to be the mean of where you are placed on in the after life no matter how much one has they will too have to answer to THEE.

And what goes around will surely come back again because this world is constantly changing you must be ready for that change just save your soul do not let anyone break it cause you will need it at those pearly gates now get ready to go home it's getting late. On the way home I made a silent vow to myself to educate me and have an unbreakable belief in me and of course people. Now five years had past and off I went to Michigan State University (MSU) where I and racism becomes up close and personal.

The year was 1975 I was a freshman at one of the largest college in the U.S. after the draw went down out of the civil rights movement came a lot of programs that aided peopled who came from low income areas such as myself but we still saw a lot of turmoil daily like the white parents coming and demands their child be taken out of the room where they was staying with blacks and professors giving black students lowers grades than others. The most shocking I can say is that they made us change majors because we came from low income areas so they felt that we were not capable of keeping up with the demands of the preferred field. Like when I came my major was prep med that is in the medical field but a university counselor told me that if I wanted to attend the school I would have to change my major because coming from a inner city high school I could not do the work required for first year premed students. I fought and arguaed but in the end I had to do what she said because all the black students were told that who came from the inner city schools. There were many thing we had to take that really frustrated us like psychology the instructor would always say at every lecture that all these finding do not relay to black people because the studies are only base on the average white male so most of the black students did not takes an interest and began to doubt why we had to major in that field anyway. So I changed my major to criminal justice where I in 1988 got a bachelor in science from the University of Houston.

You know most of that did not bother us because we stayed high yes herbs was our cure for everything it's a walk out today so give me herbs or the protesting at the student building so what give me herbs almost everything in our generation was solved or deal with in that manner because the old folk like to drink and we knew we could not think once we did liquor.

Although I was not in the south but the racism in the north was lived and hidden inside of their standards and qualifications like when I got my degree one of the Deans in the 1980's at the University of Houston was Dr. Bobbitt after finishing I saw him.

He said well congratulation Shirley that probably will be the most expensive piece of wall papers you is ever bought. I said no way what you're talking about I plan to kick some doors open with this piece of paper as hard of a time that I have getting it this should be my key to porosity and get me the best jobs to be a productive law-abiding citizen. He then said yeah that might get you in the door but now you're considered a threat and that's a dangerous position to be in because you're a bad threat so don't expect the doors to opening to wide to prosperity because the real white world still have some tricks up their sleeves for you yet.

Remembering the word's of my mother who along with the older people in my neighborhood like my granny the world is round not flat it will change you must be willing and my mother she was the most influential person in my life even though she had thirteen of us she installed believe that I install into my son and that is one must be in this world for everything not anything and one must know and over stand the differences, doing almost anything to achieve one must always know to plan and calculate to slowly find their groove then make that move now that's how the righteous leaders will rule.

So, the training of all that seeks shall be of the norms as this world continues to form. That why we must stop this ware housing of youths and place them much like in the early days of the civil rights movement of the inner cities and into training schools that enable them to really get a job paying enough wages to carry their families to the generation to come not merely giving them a basic education.

We must simply rethink our entire educational process and developed a new method of selecting homes for the masses because it will save us from being on the brink of mankind's own extinction.

Also this will make our youths of today learn a better way of thinking to not to be bringing into our society a group of younger with less animal instincts and band together in a human brotherhood to save all humanity having fewer shelters that clearly violate the human dignity of a folk which enables all mothers' cries to be heard around the United States as well as the Middle East doing always with wars and breeding no more whores. So we as this generation can leave a legacy of stability rather humility worshipping the rich and loving the wrong things in life doing away with the black codes that were designed to keep the oppress back in a darkness of despair. I stand with the word of Shakespeare, we must move across the Homeless and racial line. I summon us tax payer and elite alike and all souls to come graciously with the oppress bringing with fore a true dwelling for the better life of Americans whom strive to find some type of peaceful living for their offspring to come.

And our fore founding father such a Thomas Paine one of the original drafters of the constitution will be fore right peering from the cloud.

A world where every America and alike can bring children into a world with at least a home we all must have insight to the Promise Land and on earth make away for the Homeless man doing what in God plan America was founded on the premise that one person can try all there life to do a task and two or three united can do the same task in half the time this is a mother cry do not just let it go by...It still seems that some of the black codes that were started in the 1800's under president Andrew Jackson still have not dealt with by us as a civilized nation of people we let the inner city become run down with the white flight of the 1960's and some places like in Detroit especially the highland park area the streets are so old having the building to be places where the bird can no longer live.

We must over stand for us to rear less youths with animal instincts to just cheat or steal we must open the doors of opportunity starting in our public schools not merely teaching the basic of what they had but teach them a real trade and skill that they can carry in the real world. For the world is a circle and if we do not change our educational process now to less workshop and hair dressing and bring real technical learning into public schools along with our high paying careers we will be heading for mankind self extinction.

Leaving a legacy of greed for all simply not to try for this should be all of our cry not just a mother's but in cities like Miami, Los Angles and in Houston along Jensen street where the houses are so bad they all look like they have been hit by a hurricane of life.

And build houses that we all can afford so our legacy can be of peace and togetherness among all races of people for him our father in heaven created one race and we as civilized people labeled it the HUMAN RACE.

MANKIND'S EXTINCTION

MANKIND'S EXTINCTION

The extinction of mankind is becoming evidence because they have not learned from the prehistoric species. Modern Man belief in the survival of fitted race to control this place having not put the land first simply wanting to harm the human race.

For they are followers of greed and they will do anything to success.

But even those that live high in the hills will see that this land is not our land and they to will not be saved from going to an early grave because God see their unwise actions which do not affords all cultures a fair chance to advance. And he will not be happy for disregarding his land.

For he will not be pleased as we continue to destroyed his ocean, and the trees that causes his people not to get a cool breeze. Yes mankind may become extinct if the powers to be do not wake up and think cause NO man is an island therefore; NO man can walk along for mankind may perish but God great earth will be cherish for decades to come so all righteous people do not be afraid just watch and do not RUN.

A MOTHER'S CRY

Now, son can't you see what God intended our lives to be.
For only the strong will endure longevity.

Yes, because God cares that the elite are not fair, they too will have to come to those pearly gates, having only their good deeds to be standing, not who you hate. So, son never sit with unrighteous men who are only in this world for another hit, so Scotty can beam them up into a life of useless schemes that confuse the mind and place your life on a path of destruction, until there is no way of saving your soul. That will cause one to attack, having no way of coming back. Now son please try to listen and understand this Mother's Cry.

United we stand, divided we fall.

Seeds of Greed
Chapter 9

Remembering when I first moved to Houston feeling alone while cleaning seventeen restrooms at the University of Houston down Town College.

I met an elderly women named Ms. Mertis she was very strong in her working ethics. She had been working for the college for over ten years and if not for her wisdom I would have not gotten though to my next step in live. Nor would I have made it through the night. She must have been the first angel that comes into one life. Because she felt by pain before I told her my thoughts. One day I had a real bad head ache and did not feel like working. As she talked to me her words carried me through the rest of my life. I told her that I grew up thinking if one lived their life in accordance to there beliefs nothing nor harm would ever come to them. But not matter what I did something always got in my way. I tried to live in a righteous manner but something like proverty is my only friend. So why should we even try to better our lives, because I did not come to this state away from my friend to clean toilets and that's what I'm doing. This causing head aches alone with anxiety. She replied you might as well be living in a fishing bowl because their will always problems in your life. No one can escape problem they enable one to be alive and when they're no more problems in your life you will be dead. Your challenge in life is to over come that problem. Without causing harm to yourself and others. It's like the earth is our test in brotherhood of each other. I feel that God would have not given you this job if he felt that you did not or could not do it. Did you ever think that this job maybe the opening for another and your faith is being tested. Because many just give up and anything that worth having you will have to struggle for. That's the way of the world and as long as one lives there are problems. It's the only way we know that we are living from the problems one encouthers. Your test is how you handle these problem you heard of the saying that many are chosen but only a few are let in. This is because some gave up and they failed God's test. This world is not the final but what you do in this world enables you to be placed in the next. For instances if you were a lovers of plants then in the next world you would be caring for them. So as long as you keep fighting the odds and do not sell yourself out that is staying strong to your faith.

Ridding on your path will be hard but just give your burden to God. Once you done what ever you could. He does not want you to be a saint just know what's good and what anit. Along your path of life stay close to a manner that do not put you on an unrighteous path with your God.

Now I say this with the utmost of passion for you because that headache you have is a problem. That you must work through to remain on this job. Yes other's days will test you but you must stop thinking that the world cares. They do not and the sooner one realizes that the world do not own no one nothing but you own the world everything. For he gave his only begotten son for you to live in peace and harmony with each other. You will one day not clean floors. So you must keep to your struggle and let nothing stop you from obtaining what God placed you on earth for. Maybe not to clean but you will know from within time. If it's meant for you it will be given to you in due time. You must understand that you miss your family and friends back home. But sometimes one has to make a move in order to find what Gods plan is for them. No matter how much family one has they are going to die along. So wipe your face and stop those tears because one day you will look back and find yourself old as me and the problem will be easier to handle. Remember the storms in life test your faith because many are created but only a few are chosen.

For problems are a part of ones life do not make them a fact in your life. Work pass them because if they do not kill you they will make you stronger. If you do not fall into the devil's pit of greed and deceived. As long as we live on this earth there will be problems and how you handle them will make a better person out of you. As time goes on cause just as time it self they to will pass. Your job is to not let them break you down your soul.

Well that means I must live like a saint. No you just always know your limits and do not let no one as you young folks say turn you out. Because in everyone's life they will have a story no matter if their Homeless they will surely be obstacles that burdens our lives. But we must keep our faith and let God control our fate. So as I once again began cleaning I could hold my head up high for I knew my way of life was not wrong. I did not have to be a saint nor did I have to be perfect because the old ways of life was chancing rapidly and soon I would be on my way to a better job. Which came because I soon started working as a dispatcher for the college and did obtain a Bachelor of Science in criminal justice from that very college.

Since everyone has a story I shall now tell you mine. I lived in an one bedroom apartment on the south east side of Houston paying over six hundred dollars a month. My desire to move was strong because I wished to at least provide something for my child. One knows that as we live on this here earth as long as we have the basic then half our battle is won. Therefore instead of keep getting a landlord rich I wanted to start making plans to obtain something for my old age, I did not want to sign another lease that could pin me down more. So after traveling back to Houston we were Homeless needing time to move us out of the devil's den of shelters of lost hope.

Now we must try to understand what the old folk is saying because the world we live in is not promise to us. We all should try to live and leave something to our offspring, if it's just simply a home to live after their gone.

The government should understand that we as a people must live in this world and stop the corporate geed of having so much and giving so little.

In this world we are fighting between the religious group over who will be the ruler of the land many fail to see that we do not have to in order to live just as I was told we will always have problems but we must try more to work out our problems, without so much killing of each other and live to help our brothers of all walks of life, after all we will all died in the end.

The elite of the world makes one think their ways of the world is greed this plants a deadly seed for generation to come.

Yes, money will buy the materialism of this world. But you can't take it when your gone. I can safety say that it will not bring you happiness only give you a sense of false security. Because those friend that money bring; will surely not be with you when it gone. So we as a people must stop the killing in the Middle East and in our country. Because that's not a proper way of handling problems. For we must leave a legacy that we want our children to be proud of rather than one of greed, can't the leader of today see that's a deadly seed.

Furthermore how can we honestly say that we are a nation of the people if we do not even afford the same opportunity that gives the proper wages? That enables all to have equality to live. With some of the riches in life instead of being inherently disadvanced from birth while surviving on earth. We all do deserve a little propriety while in this world, for those whom want the chance to over come the obstacles that life will bring to you.

Some may feel that this is just wishful thinking because not everyone can succeed, I'm not talking about that fact I'm just advocating a better system that's geared most toward equality, that enable a fairer chance to advance.

Also, some may ask what gives this writer the right and the creditability to write this type of book. Because she not a certified teacher she's merely a sub.

But I can tell them that they maybe right but as I said before I was born into a world on fire, I have been in the teaching aspect of the educational system in three state for over ten years.

This give me the power from God because I have over came many problems and Stayed strong in faith not living as a saint but over standing what right and ain't. Never living to judge no one only wanting a world where we could live within a system that affords all that seek a change. Even in the testing procedures that allows one to grade with equality not just taking tests that are not fair from the start. Having unempathic tester to systematically fail one and laugh in their face or designing physiological test that merely ask questions like do you have sex with a fowl and other that are made to keep one out.

So for all those that think that I have not enough educational credentials to write this book nor any life struggles to know what's the largest problems of this generation. I say to them look at you. Just because one is educated and another may have enough life experience to live thorough the times that have tested their faith. Not giving in to the problems and letting nothing too ever bring them down. As one get older they realizes that life seem to suffer from the been their none that semdrome. So their legacy on earth in their mind and we all want to leave one that states or defines their purpose on this here earth. Just like the other ones that came here first. Now being older I just want to reach one or two people whom are trying to accomplish something. Maybe gotten to a point where the problems still come. But after they read this book they no longer want to quit or run. Because now I have over came obstacle and just I was told I like to tell all that seek the almighty will come in due time just stick to your faith.

To live in this world of wars and racism is a test of our faith. When we get to the pearly gates our past and present has been place before us. We all want to say that our life on earth was not in vein. Although we lived in a world on fire one was not taken in from the foolishness or unheartless desires. Nor did one live for only the fortune and fame but overstood that the creator created one race and we as people labeled it the human race.

For to live in this world of greed and cooperate deceived we must keep a firm understanding in what we believe...

Yes, may that be the reason that good news makes one rejoice to form clear thoughts. For a prudent heart that is sorrowful will truly live to see tomorrow.

Cause into everyone's life their will definitely be Sorrows.

SORROWFUL HEARTS

Sorrowful Hearts
Chapter 10

Once back when at the age of 10 years old my mom was watching the funeral of Dr. King on our black and white television. She was crying shouting that the poor folks would have to suffer much longer because our leader was dead and the struggle would be harder. I then asked why he was so important. And she replied that in life we all have duties to perform and his duties was to insure that all who wanted got a fair chance at obtaining opportunities within our rims of dreams. So we all did not have to suffer at the bottom. He died for all people to be in life's circle with the proper means to accomplish our dreams. He was a man that saw God purpose for us before any man and made it his mission to enable all to see the wicket man ways. Now they have made a martyr out of him so he's live forever. The circle will be fulfilled using his memory. The road to economic equality will surely come having the have and the have not to clash just a little longer. Because they can kill off a man but they can never kill off reality and the reality is that one can not take the world with them when there gone through those pearly gates. So you must stand strong in your life you see, my child no matter how much one has we are all going to die in the end. So, why they do not want us to have anything and why do we feel that we can not have finder things in live it's just beyond me…Yes sometimes I feel that it's us poor who are afraid of change because most of us do not enforce in our children the important of a good education. We trend to leave it up to the schools. Having no time or if their child does not learn they blame it on the teacher because they did not teach. When the teachers' are so heavy burden with the paper work and the testing aspect. They can only do what's the state and or school broad has mandated for them to teach. The time went teachers could teach has been washed away in the money game. Because if the students do not score high on these standardized test then there school funds are cut short. The teacher is looked upon as if they are bad teacher's. Making the day's when one could teach to be a thing of the past. Having Dr. King ideals of this world to be still a simple dream.

Then morning aroused and my sister Mary Janice who we called MaryJ went out to get some food as we walked we saw broken glass all over the streets.

The stores were looted just like a sale but all prices were smacked.

The police and the nation guards were patrolling but they could not stop the looter because they did not want to kill children. Once we were in a shoe store and the guard made us get out before we could pick up anything we were so scared that we went home. And once we arrived our older brothers had everything it was like Xmas. But after the riot unlike in LA the store never did reopen in parts of Detroit and I guess it like my mom would say the circle has began to turn because the history book would read that the riot of 1967 of the 100 riots that broke out Detroit had the worst having over 40 or so people to die. So while in the 1990 LA riot after another man in the center named King I knew that the circle was turning again even though he was not a leader but realizing that ever 10 years or more the brick just get a little to thick meaning the oppress get a little tied of the nonsense of our leaders and act out in civil disobediences. They become depress and are stress from being enconomically, politcally disenfranchised that completely leaves them out of the corporate mainstream of this society.

As the civil rights movement of the 1970's processed the number of minorities mainly African Americans increased from 20% in 1960's to 40% by the end of the decade. Having the ladder part of the 1990's to be less concern with the movement in general doing away with most of the programs that seemed to bring about a change.

However, the 1990's made some gain in the number of African Americans who were below the poverty line to 79% above but there is a 31% of them still living below the line of poverty level. But the 1970's brought about a difference in the type of racism that we as a nation of people face today.

This was made clear to me as I finished college and begin my journey of professional employment.

Although the 1970's brought about programs that enabled many minorities seeking higher education an opportunity to attend universities and monetary assistances in federal and state grants and loans. Also, brought about gains in African American who were below poverty line to a 31 percent of them still living below poverty and there were an increased enrollment in colleges and universities that ensured that they would likely have higher paying jobs than in the 1960's but sure enough the blacks codes started at the end of slavery still exist. Because as I finished college much of what the dean told me was true being the expensive piece of wall paper that I ever brought because many of the higher paying jobs just let one fill out the application and that it. You see those words never bother me but the various people who said thing like my sociologist professor such as Dr. Laine who taught in the late 1980's in Houston who told me from one conversation about the inside prejudices that our generation must fight today. Remembering that I was thinking that she was crazy because racism was gone and there were never anything such as black codes. She would say there is still racism but now it more hidden and hard to detect. Now that you are through with the upper level education do not think the doors of employment will be open to you whole heartily. I could not stop thinking of that each time I did not pass an exam like once for the sheriff department where there were over four hundred question or more of things like do you like your mother, do you have sex with animals, do you have sex with dogs, do you have sex with a fowl and so on.

Once it was checked even if it was no pass or fail the examiner said that I did not pass and he would not recommend me for hiring because I had fly away personality. When I asked what was that I was told that cause I was not from this state it was very likely that I would not remain in this state and that was in 1989. Another time I tried to take the law school admissions test and I had a hard time passing even after I'd taken a class to prepare. I then went to one of the dean at the time and he told me that I was having such a hard time because it was meant to be hard to keep minorities out of their law schools. He said laughingly that a group of old white men gotten together and asked now how can we keep these people out and they developed the LSAT. I replied your joking now tell me how to pass.

He replied there is no pass or fail like many of the test you just must score high and the test was design for you not to because much of the materials do not apply to people of color. The materials on many of the test for employment applies to the white population standards of life styles and that pretty much was the basic of how this nation was founded. A group of old white men got together and ask themselves how can we presver the office of presidency.

I left his office in tears and every state like Los Angeles I tried to take the CBEST many time and never passed and the test for other professional jobs having one examiner laugh in my face after she checked it saying you missed it by one point ha-ha come back in six months.

So now I am stuck being a substitute teacher and many people and students say why you don't be a real teacher or you have a college degree and you work for less pay. While the principal makes all the money and do not even deal with the kids. I just silently walk away and continue to put in application because I gotten to old to even care.

You see as I age! I know my soul have been saved because this world of fire that I have been born in is constantly changing.

Also, what we fear the most is our selves and being treated with less at the bottom for their never ever wilt there be a time again which allowed the slavery of a people to settle in.

As Dr laine said this inside racism will fade because the world not flat it's a circle and it will change.

So the people in New Orleans must not be afraid for nothing and no one will remain the same that a fact of life and the dead have paid the price.

SORROWFUL HEARTS

Sorrow is a device that allows ones soul to refrain from being bold. May that be the reason that killing of one another will never go out of this region.

For anger, not love rules our heart causing a rotten of our bones. Having many people to follow a path of envious thoughts.

Which allows them to release sorrowful idea's of ways just to cheat, or steal.

Foolish is the man that do not give knowledge nor wisdom a chance.

Always wanting to dispense hasty wicked actions of constantly hunting.

Giving everyone that they encounter no mercy.

For they will not have the final say.

Yes, even the anger envious souls will have to mend their ways if they want to live out their days.

Yes, may that be the reason that one must teach their sons and daughters wear the crown of a prudent man not greed or designer clothes.

Now, may that be the reason that the killing of another is so very Godly wrong, No matter what side of the tracks they live on.

Now, just let me get some sleep and if you need me just come to Venice Beach and ask around for PAPA JOE ok everyone will know.

PAPA JOE

Papa Joe
Chapter 11

Out of the dark corners of mostly every inner city struggling unlovely building and the homeless people loaf leisurely inside these dwelling.

Particularly in Miami and Detroit where the buildings are so old only the smell of decay having a place for just the birds to lay there nest not fit for humans to rest making the geographical grounds of the of the homeless to rise constantly. They can be seen for miles in cities like Miami having the center of town so run down one is afraid to walk the street even in day light hours.

Where as Detroit the city is so run down the casinos are a sub city within there major city having nothing around such as outside business that the people who live in Detroit can built upon.

Causing the population to live among the thrown down shabby structure that have been standing for decades. In both of these cities the shelters are much filled with HIV clients and abusers of controlled substances that there is hardly any room for the neither homeless mother nor children. Having one to be addicted to drugs in order to receive immediate attention for assistances. While we were in Miami several people informed us of there policy of helping the abusers\rather than mothers and children saying hit the pipe then they will help you as the rain came down my son and I just tried to obtain assistance at the salvation army in Miami and a worker told us that her hands was tied with everyone other than families and right now in her city they have over 10 thousand women and children left out having to stay into motel because they have no room and most can not afford the high rent of an apartment. So, she made some call and give us ten dollars out of her own pocket and send us to Ft. Lauderdale after a worker at downtown shelter told us that we were not Miami problem cause we were only there for five days and we landed in Ft Lauderdale first. Therefore, we should go back there and become there problem but once arriving there the people were so mean it seen their souls were lost no one smiled they all walked around with a sad look upon their face we felt we better try to get back to Houston where at least I had a job. Because when we did find a shelter they were even stricter than Houston having not to get a room because a non nurse give me a drug test and said I did not pass because I had weed in my system two months ago and it stays for ninety-days where cocaine only stays for 72 hours. So their drugs of choice is that not weed and they shelters are filled with those type of abusers. Which is their right to check a person out but why do they must go inside of a persons private pleasures of life because crack heads had made the whole world not trusting of people in general. We all know from the beginning of time some of the great men of our world use several of stimulus having them on a relaxation basic like Stigma Freud and other if one study their history. For God creates the world so we as a people can use but pay a heavy price if one abuse having all these wars over a plant but allowing places like Michigan and California to decriminalizes the use of such plants. Which enables the authorities to concentrates their effort on the serious problem of job training and the Homeless instead of state sending funds on testing and drugs wars and leaves people to live in shabby street built years ago having the baby boomers generation of the 1970's not seeing our present world going in the direction that they fought all their life to prevent. Which are rights granted in our Bill of Rights because our leaders of today fail to see and center their funds not on the things in this world the built us as a nation but matters that infringe on people personal freedom towards a plant that only bring about a temporary stimulus of self satisfaction. But somewhere with the passage of time our leaders got lost and forgotten what's really important and the goodness of our brothers that why we have some of the saddest days of our lives like on 9/11 remembering the day after as I was on Vince beach I ran into a old man who lived on the beach for many years and the conversation we had I put in a poem using his name as the title Papa Joe.

As the waves were coming harshly up on the shore we both knew the Gods' were angry at the world he said because we as a civilized nation has taken much of the forgiveness and kindness out of this world. Having the ocean to be his great big aquarium and he sits right at the ocean sitting right there drinking his magic potion.

Remembering in the year of 1975 as I came out of high school while attending college I became very upset with my school because I still was told that I could not write and made to take all of my English classes over. She said, coming from an inner city publish school that I would not be ready for the premed course therefore, I should change my major to psychology or business.

So I listen and change to psychology where at that time they did not do any studies on blacks because the professor kept reminding all the blacks in the class. Most of us had a hard time even passing the courses because we had to learn an entire new way of understanding college materials having many to simply drop out period.

As writer like Dr. Jesse Glassor a retired economic professor at Texas Southern University once wrote in his book called "Breaking the chains of Poverty" we must try to stop the cycle of welfare dependency and provide more funds into training.

That more true today than ever because many of the schools on the high school levels just have the traditional vocational skills trade such as cosmology or wood shop but unlike some of the northern schools that do have construction or computer repairs and various of other trades that help students while completing high schools.

However there is a strong need to add training in their present curriculum instead just teaching the basic over again causing our policy makers to rethink our present educational process to fit more of today's student needs.

They must not just continue to test in order to obtain funding but enable the business to come and let some students intern more rather than test because some students are not obtaining the proper means to at least get a job paying enough wages to take care of themselves once they are out of high school and studies show that only a small percent of our population has even completed a higher educational institution the nations homeless shelters could be rearranged to fit the modern day society and the educational systems can organized to be in accordance to the students training needs so all that want can find employment that pay enough wages that enables them to care for the demands of adulthood.

As in 1862 from the days of reconstruction under President Lincoln whom office enacted the thirteen amendment which was passed that abolished slavery there where black codes that were enacted under President Andrew Johnson administration that are still exist today. These codes varied from state to state but prevented African American and other minorities from achieving social, political and economic equality. Along with the mainstream of our society. Even today the public schools systems are clearly unequal for instances as I substituted in the various of state like Houston and Los Angeles one could see the difference by the run down buildings and the lack of technologies training that were available in the inner cities schools and the absent of parent involvement in the policy making process. This is properly why the schools have remained the same for decades due to this lack of inner city lower income complaint process.

This is either because of one or more reasons which are that the oppress people think that their voices will go unheard and there is no reason to compliant because they will fall on death ears. But in order to break the cycle of poverty this country must provide training that will allow the inner city youth that wish to obtain jobs the means not just housing them in school building that can not properly prepared to give them the adequate job training nor placement facility. They could rearrange our present educational systems much like earlier days to fit their modern needs. Much like in the 1970's which gave business the opportunity to adopt a high school and place senior or juniors on actual paying jobs have them intern at the school while still in their school to get training in the field.

Similar to what some Detroit school do now and very few southern schools do but on a higher level than public schools. This could make places like ITT part of their everyday courses for the student and employer to better adapt to each other.

The school can do a search to find the top profession and provide test along with materials that help them actually learn to work on a job this could move us in an upward direction rather than the continued process of students who are at schools like Jones High school in Houston where the law makes them come to class and the teacher teaches them the required lessons but they can not seem to apply it to an actual job.

Also, this would give students more choices when finished with their educational process.

Some people may say well how come these people think that their ideas will work they are just a person whom only became a substitute teacher and they never really worked in the real arena of teaching however if I have not addressed that manner in a humane way let me explain a little story that brought me through some bad times in my life.

The year was 1980 and like most teenagers we never truly believed that there was a real God because why would he or she allow so much racism and hate to occurred. Surly this thing called God was merely an escape coat that the older people called upon in their times of trouble because all they did was call upon him in bad times.

I myself did not think God was true until I enrolled in a religion course at Lansing Community college I found more than an understanding of God.

I wrote my journey in a play called in search of my soul which is a story about a young girl on a quest to find God and in turn found her soul.

So from that I can say that God live in side of us all and the underlying basic of the play is to enable reader to understand life's purpose. For them to not get lost nor wicket in their journey through their own life and times. On that personal quest to find their soul...we must just make sure that we are right like Michael Jackson once said look at that man in the mirror make sure you are doing what you suppose to be doing when God comes for your soul.

So people because there know big title behind my name remember all he ask of us is to save our selves and nothing else. Having this world to be our test in our true brotherhood in mankind that do not cause us to become extinct nor put us in a bind.

Therefore, since we all have a story to tell or if mines could enable at least one person some comfort then my job is done and his will in me has been fulfilled.

For titles will not mean anything when we are called to that final curtain.

Now in the words of my dear mother we all must live in this circle of life with a purpose. Not caring who came first only living until he calls us trying to be in this world giving with kindness doing his will not the devil's deeds for God has his breed.

So, I say to people like my sister, God made me write this book. From the experience that he put before me because I learned form and if I could share them with the world he made it possible. Just to give the oppress a voice and leader another choice to lead the people into the future with dignity.

After all he was a simple carpenter and he dies for us all not only the title holder. Let this be the reason for my book to be the means to heal a hurting soul before him. As we are called to our next phrase in our lives. As in my play I saw a place where the people who worked at a company controlled their own wealth and in turn they obtain excellent health and what one did on earth was their means of being placed. It was described to me as being external life and on earth one must make the right sacrifice to be granted the means to come live among the kings and queens not greed nor their riches on earth only helping their fellowman when ever one can.

While traveling being accompanied by a voice in the clouds instructing me to go and seek my purpose and I may return to paradise.

This was a major factor in returning to this placed known now to me as the promise land.

PAPA JOE

Sitting looking at the ocean with his old face filled with emotions.

Replying lightly "live and let other's live" that is how this world should be just as the wave brushed upon the surface.

Yes, the Gods are angry this morning as we sat and watched the roughness of the tide coming briskly on the sand.

You see the Gods are our ancestors and they see that the devil has taken much of the LOVE and WISDOM out of the world.

Having plenty of badness that can't be suppressed.

Because certain races want to remain on top and each side will destroy much of this place before we all stop and live with grace.

So, one just becomes fed up with the ills of the world and simply spends time just drinking their magic potion right here at this ocean. For this is my great big aquarium that takes my mind back to travel to the time when love was the spice of life and many did see that wisdom were the vehicles that would lead the rulers. Yes, I'll keep resting my mind on the good times when we all did what we could for our fellowman whenever we had something to share having those day to be very rare.

Yes now, that's why the ocean is my aquarium so, I must say the hell with them.

MY POPS

Since I was a baby my Pops put bottles in my mouth whenever I was crying. My Mom teaches me things while I'm young and like the fish learning to swim in the ocean my Pop and Mom taught me with devotion.

Although Y'all met on a big ship called the Cavalier and I have not seen you near.

My Pop is still the top of my brain that I will forever hold down inside.

Dad loves Mom and God.

My Pops
Chapter 12

Now this part of the book has the title of My pops because I felt that it was very important in describing my failed attempt finding true love because send everyone has a story I only told half of mine.

For me my life being as I moved to New Orleans and met my husband.

Sometimes that old folk saying is careful of what you pray for cause you just might get it was truer for me than ever.

You see, most of the time I did not believe in anything that was not real because I felt by nature I was a realist. Meaning all things happen for a reason.

So once a friend ask me to go with her to New Orleans to a Communication event I was more than happy because I pray for a man that was my Mr. Right.

Her name was Jackie and she was a native Britain but was dissented from Jamaica along with her family. She because my first stepping stone on my path in pursuit happiest. One day while in New Orleans she stood up showing off her tall big frame with black hair that she offends spent hours braiding. She said as we were getting dressed Hey do you think that you would ever get married as she put on her red dress sitting down to put on matching shoes and the earring's reply hell girl if I find a man that I have been praying for, then she said what that some one who's rich and fine like my man.

Now girl I want one that do not sell drug, nor use and positive who wants something in life and do neither chase women nor men and just had a strong potential I would married in a heart beat. Just then I finished dressing wearing a white tightly fitted dress and we both laugh and said let's go have fun.

Well hours later I meant a short man with the most strange looking eyes and golden yellow skin. We danced the night away and as it became time for us to go we exchanged phone numbers and began communicating.

He later sent money for me to come back and not wanting to go along naturally I asked my friend to accompany me on the trip.

Once arriving we got closer and I decide to move there as stayed in New Orleans for two years then we moved to my home state of Detroit Michigan.

The year was 1995 after we had been married for four years I was pregnancy with my only son. The marriage became bitter because one could easily see that Nigel wanted out so one day I enter the kitchen of my sister's house where we were staying and I saw a green piece of paper on her floor.

Thinking to myself that this must be a bill because it little likes a receipt from a purchase. So, I picked up the paper and unwrapped it and the note read, Mommy I want to run away from home because I can no longer stay here with him.

Coming to a complete shock I seamed and my sister ran into the room asking what's wrong. Falling to my knees I could not speak and she grasped the note out of my hand and started shouting I will kill him that's my daughter she is only eight years old.

I said wait a minute you do not know that it him for sure because another friend is named Nigel. She said well call that fucker and if it's not him I will apolized but their was no need for her to do that. After I called his at work he admitted to the fact and said that it was my fought because I left him along with her. I replied that you are a sick fucker and a person who can not stand nor no your own mistakes. Because I suspected that something was up when you would tell me that she needed money to buy her personal items and the boy's did not. Also, you sick bastard when I was in Jamaica I caught you in the gym with that ten year old. But fool you are not in your country where you men get away with shit like that you're in America and we do not like sex offender okay. Mean while my sister comes in with a number of boy and they started to beat on him knocking him to the ground lastly she pick' up a large sized rock and holds up her hand to throw it just then I grabbed her hand looking her face to face as she tells me to move, Well, you're be the one that explains to him why you killed his daddy. She then stopped and said just get that fucker out of my house but he was already gone running so fast that I did not know he was out of the house until a girl friend called me and asked me what was the matter because he was at her house and a lot of people were at her door and she could not understand a word he was saying. I told her to hold him their and I would explain once I arrived.

Now after all the drama went down and I had my son I tried to stay with him but the trust and loyalty were gone and once that destroyed two people can call it over.

Therefore, after ten year later I talked to our son and there is something I guest about a boy and their dad because no matter how much single parents explain in details they are still longing for that side of their genetics makeup.

So, when people say to not listen to there children I say listen.

In order for your child to remain whole and to grow in this world with less anger you as a parent must close all door that lead to self destruction for the world will be vastly unfair and no one will really care if one falls off.

Also, I did not want my child to be saying these words the last time that I saw my dad I was two years old and I truly wanted to teacher.

Having to accept my role in life as a substitute teacher and nothing else.

Because after I worked with children I know that we live in a world that controls the races by standardized test and maybe this is far enough for me to go because as I said before I was born into a world on fire and for now all I aspire to be is a substitute teacher.

Now this is my reason for telling this part of my life for everyone will have a story and as times goes on one must make dam sure that they are ready.

And ones life will be guided by the choices one take that will steer the path you make. I chose the man know one told me to go to another country and find a love.

You see unlike Stella I lost my groove once I wedded a Jamaica not saying that they are all bad but remember they go by the Old Testament much like American man you know the one that reads do as I say not as I do.

So be true to God and love thyself.

SEEDS OF GREED

Yes, it appears that our society have planted the Seed that breeds greed among the old and young. It has became imbedded into the fabric of our society having many to feel that materialism is the key to happiness. You all must see that for other generation to come the seed of greed must stop being rooted into the minds of the old and young.

Because for to many years we have shown them so much of the life styles of the rich and famous and hardly ever allowed them to over stand the life's styles of the shameless

A WATER DRIFT

Sea shells in the water. Once upon a time there was a man picking up shells at the sea. He found a pearl in one he told all the people that one must believe in Yourself.

Then one can find hope that opens your heart and one will be smart, and kind. So, just as the sea shells in the water one must mend their soul to stop from being picked too soon like the seashells and the moon.

The Saddest Hours
Chapter 13

As the incidents kept occurring in each state having to leave moving to California in the city of LA in which we loved but the more I kept taking the exam for teaching the more I kept failing. So, after the 5th time I decide to move back to Houston proving that I did not have fly away personality but the desire to become what God brought me into the world to do and if It was simply to teach then I just had to settle for that in any capity that was given to me open at these trying times.

Also if my degree was an expensive piece of wall paper then I would use it to teach because we as substitute teachers' are more than just babysitters. We do teach classes seeing the type of racism that Dr. laine spoke about are stronger today than ever. Because most people do see it or they do not care. Now as I reach into my middle age all one can do is know that their soul is been saved and still try to install a strong self will into our children. That could enable them to move pass the barriers and onto a life that necessary for them to succeed and pray that one day I will be born into a world where my color is not a factor in my life but a fact of my life.

Because although we have the less paying job in the educational system we are valuable part of the process. We will be for decade to come.

We deal with all types of adminstrations, students, and we can tell where the good schools and teachers, principals and lunches. What schools give us the proper break as some if not most feel that we do not need a break and some put us in more than one class a day and we must accept it or not come back to the school.

Because we can be fired or asked not to come back for any reason or no reason at all.

It's like we fight a war at every school that we attend because the teacher's aid do not like us and constantly give us no assistances and because we hold four year college degree, not a teaching certificate.

Where as the janitors, the clerks the cafeteria worker and aids do not have any but<**>

We are only lacking that certificate and most of us know that if one has attended a four year university we can teach a class room but it's the way of this world to keep us down to limit the amount of people in the high paying fields.

Because some classes that I've been to the aid does not know what it takes to get a college degree. They can not help the students on that level.

So, when people ask me why I just sub I say it's a job and I must feed myself and son.

For them to think that a non degreed person should be paid more than a college graduate is just the way of this world and maybe in the next one they will see us for not just being a sub but, a teacher. A person that been through the bad and made it in life whole as time unfolded.

Today's modern world according to some of the history books are changing such as the one at schools in states like at some middle schools. As in elementary middle and some charter schools in Detroit Michigan.

One can view there books and find that the history today we learned that the world circle is getting smaller because of technology has help to shrink our world.

Having people to grow and become closer than ever before.

Also, the chance of people meeting different culture of people has become increasable greater with the global network of computers linked to the internet. Having people of many races to face each and learn most about their world than they did in the pass making racism less common in our near future.

Therefore, learning to understand and respect each cultures will become even more stronger because through this global network personal computers will have stronger processing power than those of the 1960's that simply just help place Americans on the moon.

Today the internet is use by millions of people use to exchange all types of information like mail shop, do research, play games with people all over the countries making the world seems to be much smaller.

This also can become a dangerous tool because we've become a world that do not believe in people we've become a world that love and depends on computers.

No matter what we may say, if the computer says so chances are that one will not take your word. But the computer like, if the computer says that you have a ticket no matter what you say the computer will put one in jail. For no reason at all. And only ones hard earned fund can get you out.

But all in all we became better people because of computer for more information can be found out about matters of our concern. Like the leaders have to be more honest than before because we now can find out thing about them that they use to be able to hide.

And our world has became a little smaller for there are no more cover or convert actions that do not take years to uncover. Having boggler to place them on their web site exposing them in the matter of minutes.

So, today's racism is some what less hidden as computer have become a necessary but pleasant evil.

Making our world seem a little smaller but enabling us to deal with the everyday pressures of just growing old. Remember as my mom would say that the world is a circle and once you've been around it do your time and find your place to learn to live into this world with a heavenly grace.

As our ancestor before us pass on to our children at least the means to have a simple thing such as a home.

OF the Passing to the Only-Born
O son you are my only begotten
My heart that sing and the soul that I bring
The voice of the child's blood weeps for
Who has remembered Him?
O summers maybe forgotten but thy strengthen

Comes in the end when we forget our past sin repent and we are born again.

Now just as we all must ban together to fight this new kind of war which suicide plots leveled the world trade center's twin towers in 2001, batter a U.S. warship the USS Cole in 2000, destroyed the U.S. embassy in 1998 in Nairobi, Kenya, in Saudi Arabia blew up a housing unit for U.S. troops in 1996 and struck down Oklahoma city we must stop this inside saddle racism in America.

Because foreign terrorists are coming for our youths who live in these run down shelters and thrown down hoods that this present system do not seem to care about and has simply left them out of our corporate world.

They are not only lashing out at Americans since 1983 in places like Spain, or in 1985 bombing that killed at least 18 on a U.S airbase. But they are killing Americans in places such as Scotland where a Pan Am jetliner killed 270 and in Germany in 1986 where a bomb exploded killing 3 at a Disco.

One must see from all those killings the people that did this are not stopping to see if they are black or any other race because they are killing them as Americans.

While we as a country is discriminating against the very culture of people who will protect us all.

You see we must realize that no matter how far down the road we all came as being wrong.

We must and will also continue to fight as a brotherhood of races over standing that our God made one race of people and we call them the human race.

We will remain a nation of immigrants having much ethnic diversity in this country.

We in the United States are full of people from many different lands.

Who are attracted to America by our concept of freedom and economic opportunity?

With the first Americans who developed ways to use local resources around A.D. 1500 having the colonist's settlers building a Federal Republic in the mid-1700's forming our representative democracy.

Having our first period of growth in the 1800 to 1900 as we grew from 13 states along the Pacific ocean making the early 1900's one of the leading economies in the world.

Causing the African American ethnic group who has struggled to achieve equality in America and of all cultures such as the native Americans like the Africans Americans along with the Hispanics have endured many years of economic injustice.

But there pride remains strong and their loyalties remain in American because they and their ancestors have fought in every war since the civil war.

Some like poets Simon Ortiz and Langston Hughes have written on this subject and I like to end this book using their thoughts as I see them today.

In the 1940; s-60; s they wrote words similar in meaning

Simon J. Ortiz

Survival we know
Struggles we grow
Mountains we climbed
Waiting with the passage of time
Stories we tell as we travel
Passing on to our love ones
Teaching them from birth
About the ways of this here earth

Langston Hughes

America I Sing
Although I'm Black
They hide by codes
But I will continue to struggle.
Till I get equality is all to breed
My offspring's to remain honest
and strong to live so tomorrow as
the Terrorist comes to bomb I
will fight
And not be ashamed for I see how
Beautiful we all became for our
Beloved country shall not remain
The same
America I sing
Black Codes halters
my dreams.
Still I will continue
to struggle.
Breeding my offspring
to struggle
untill theirs equality
for all.
Remaining honest and
strong.

Now we must close the gap fixing a problem that began 200 years ago.

Having the New Zealanders three answers to help to be the solution, they called them Maoris to have the skills they need to succeed and they want the pay Iwi. For land their ancestors lost.

That to me seems to be the prescription for success which will close the gap in the Homeless world as well as helping all cultures that desires in skills, wages, housing and health care.

Finally we must remember as my mom said that the world is a circle it's not flat and it will change nothing and no one will remain the same.

You must over stand that's it no matter how far and long we came down the wrong road.

We should see that computers will get us closer and it is never ever too late to turn our world around and go back down the righteous road.

This must be our generation legacy we must leave one of togetherness with all cultures of people.

Because we all fought and die as Americans in all of our wars.

So, why not let us live in America as one nation undividable with liberties and justice for all.

The Promise Land

Oh Lord of us all and king of king.

Please can you take us to a land that's not viewed by most where righteousness is their best. Equality reaped peaceful existences having no majority rules to keep us down in our schools. Because in this land justice and Equality is for everyman. Having leaders to lead with clear crystal visions making righteous decisions regardless of race only love surrounded this place. Allowing all to achieve their best so there souls can rest. Yes, in the promise land we'll automatically free to simply live peaceably.

Mirror Odyessy 1998 Darlen <**>
by Darlene Winbush June <**>

THE SADDEST HOURS - September 11, 2001

NOW, everyone must say that the morning of September 11, 2001 was the Saddest hours of our entire lives, because as the planes came tumbling down it made the world frown. For these are trying times that will not end until all denominations can live in unity or we will have mutiny.

Having the earth regress back to the prehistoric age that destroys the universe, leaving nothing behind only skulls and bones for the generations to study on.

For if there is no equality there surely will never be any peace not in the United States nor the Middle East.

Now who's the blame should be ashamed for causing so much drama that killed thousands. Ironically it was written on the walls just like a time bomb ready to fall.

THE WAR

The bombing in the buildings when I saw that, I was shocked. Because of the lost of innocent lives.

The people who did this are laughing at America and so many lives were lost.

They have caught the suspects that know the reason for this to happen

For this war can only produce bad things. Unlike Pearl Harbor, this war will hit us harder than we ever thought before; we catch the masterminds and criminals that are at fault.

THE END

Now, what exactly do the powers that be want the END of this civilization to see?

Will there be many trees, clean oceans, or star moon lighted nights. My God, many people lives perished under the watchful eyes of the nation.

Yes, by way of modern television many witness the death of thousands of innocent lives instantly crumble.

Oh rulers of all nations let's stop and do not be impatention that allow foolish acts be the blame for leaving the next generation only body parts and scattered remains.

Hello, I like to take this time to say that this play was originally written in 1983 after the author went through a Utopic pregnancy. Presently she realized that life circle had not finished evolving because she could not understand the cycles in life that turns constantly and no one can perform or created until it God's time. So, we all must treat our life like drinking a fine wine having nothing to happen before it's time. Also, a portion of the proceeds from this book will go to our nonprofit organization to help a commercial facility obtain our computer center. Now, with No further ado the founders of Adult Assistance Program Training center, Incorporated, (ADAPT, INC.) brings you a look at the mystical side of life for us righteous souls to prevail in the mitts of this living Hell.

Place: The action occurs in a hospital, classroom, clubs and church. The location of the scene is Lansing Michigan.

Time: The setting is winter in December two weeks before Xmas having the clothing attire wintery.

Disclaimer" this book/play is based on actual events, dialogue and certain events and characters contained in this book/play were created for the purposes of dramatization.

The play entitled" in Search of My Soul" is about a teen who do not believe in the existence of God, Moreover; she starts to question the entire concepts of religion in general.-So, after a major operation she falls into a comma where for sixteen days taken on a journey through Heaven then is suddenly dissented to Hell.

The expositive characters are Sheri Davis and her Jamaican dreadlock guide. Who becomes instruct mental in her reforming her faith in the religious world?

The rising action occurs when she's dropped in to a world of darkness where she's left alone. Conflicts arise when she's told that she must teach a group of unruly students to believe or she'll remain in Hell forever. Therefore; she must learn to quickly overcome obstacles in order to master the art of teaching before she can return to live everlasting. Moreover; she must not adapt the tempting behavior of friends met along the way who lower her into their deviant behaviors. The climax of the play is when she run into her sister who on her way upstairs and gives her the advice she needs to master her ability to teach that awoke her spiritual being. This allowed her to renew her faith with God.

The play ends with her allowing her students to read and recited poems originally written by them. She would began each day with at least two or more such as entitled like "A Substitute's Prayer," "A Hell's Walk, Through child's eyes and other's. Suddenly the dreadlock appeared to inform her that she will be returned to earth to seek her purpose or she will be doomed in Hell with the Boweavos forever. Also, she must steer clear of materialistic obeccssion and remain Forgiving and Kind simply leaving regent along with revenge to the lord.

Finally, after she read the last poem she saw the sparkle brighten in their eyes as if a light was turned on unblocking years of hate. From that a bond was built that allowed her to teach without any interruptions.

In Search of My Soul

A Farce in Three Acts

ACT ONE
Scene I: Early Morning
Scene II: Afternoon
Scene III: Evening

ACT TWO
Scene I: Late Evening
Scene II Next Day Morning
Scene III: Afternoon

ACT THREE
Scene I: Late Evening
Scene II: Later that Night
Scene III: Early Morning

In Search of My Soul

A Farce in Three Acts

Characters: In order of Appearances;

Sheri Davis:——————Young Dark shinned black female medium built short curly hair

Professor:——————Mr. Smith Middle-aged white male slim built long bread

Doctor: ——————Mr. John's older ball head slim built chief sergeant.

Social Worker: ——————Ms. Ruby Middle-aged white female heavy built brown long hair.

Nurse: ——————White female short blond hair slim built.

Dreadlock: ——————Tall black male long braided gray and black hair.

Students: ——————First group are Adults of all races.

Friend: ——————June Parker short mixed race female slim built short hair.

Friend: ——————Angela Jones short Mexican female medium long hair.

Friend: ——————Tony Wills short mixed race male medium built.

Friend: ——————Norman Miller tall white male slim built.

Friend: ——————Charles Wright tall black male ball headed.

Sister: ——————Darlene Win bush short black female slim built.

Students: ——————Second group are of all ages and races.

Preacher: ——————All of various religious sects, race and denominations.

Extra: ——————group in classrooms, yard, club, and church of all races.

ACT ONE

Scene I

Early Morning

The curtain rises on a classroom filled with students of various races. They are seated facing instructor at desk. Instructor enters wearing jeans and a tee-shirt center stage at podium facing students begins his lecture. Note :(students are dressed wintery).

Instructor: Hello! For all those who want to know. I'm Mr. Smith and this is religion course number 105. We will be covering (5) major denominations of religious sects. Staring with Hinduism, Buddhism, and Christianity, Jewish and Islamic philosophies in order for you to develop your own ideas of what role it plays in our everyday lives. Now, class you will not be tested on their ideologies but there underlined principles that dominated their overall philosophies. So, let's begin with the Hindu believe their mostly from India and feels that one must live a life of obedience in order to be reincarnated. The Buddhist follower feels that one can chant their way into heaven and/or to ward off bad charm. Whereas some followers of Jewish faith may believe in a type of messiah. Whereas Christians followers may think that their Lord and savior Jesus Christ was the only true God and the Islamic faiths there God Allah was the only real savior. However; they all share something in common that is some type of messenger came to spread the word of the importance for us all to lead purposeful life.

Moreover; you must form your own basic beliefs and understand that all religions are basically stating similar interpretations of what role it has played in their lives.

They all say that a certain type of messenger was sent down to earth to provide a healing and a better way of life to its followers. You see, as man evolved there was no written words. They had nothing for people to follow so the ancient followers began to draw figures leaving their marking in caves and was later transformed into the first Bible called,

'The Egyptian Book of the Dead.' However; the oldest religion recorded was in the Hindu culture and they probably have the best argument to attract followers.

Now, class for this course remember mainly all religious does is provide us is a better way of living understand that in all beliefs there is a specific type of messenger who came to help people from various region why it's important to our conscience thoughts in order, for them to live a purposeful existence in our present day society.

Now, class this completes my lecture for today are there any questions.

Sheri Davis raises her hand.

Sheri: If God is our conscious thought how he can be so powerful.

Instructor; Well, it an undefined power that held inside our bodies to allow one to cope in their times of need.

Sheri: Then religion merely an escape coat for old people in times of need.

Instructor: Well, say that but it can provide hope to anyone that desires regardless of age.

Sheri; Yes, if he can then why have the needs nor desire of blacks been heard and all this racism and greed become so rampant.

Instructor; I can't answer that because I'm not God but what I can say is that temptation is the root of mankind desires and finding our balance with God will help supply our needs.

Sheri; Now, can you answer this is there any truth in the concept of Heaven or Hell.

Instructor; I do not know that either because no one has ever came back to give the world factual evidences on their existence.

But for the purposes of this course let stay on track with the religious philosophies.

Sheri; Okay but one more question. Can you say God's is for all races or is it just an imaginary source for us to escape to when time get hard.

Instructor; Yes I can, for all that believe young lady you must understand no matter what religion you follows that he's not of mortal being it's one conscious thoughts that lives inside to keep one righteously whole while there journey in life unfolds to keep one Soul intact as they find their purpose.

Sheri; That's why he and religion are one in the same being okay with one person being born into wealth were as another to be born without even home.

Instructor; Now, all I'm stating is that God and religion gives one a form of healing and hope to cope with the internal world

It's an absolute power meaning it holds all powers absolutely. All you have to understand is that God provide us with a personal interpretation of his power that cannot be destroyed and us all poses. Lastly, we are all controlled by this power using our conscience guide our Spiritual being. That all see you next weeks.

curtain

ACT ONE

Scene II

While at home studying before going to work She thought how foolish of the instructor for not answer all of her questions. He should know if God had great power than why it can't stop all the racism and the other unrighteousness in this world. Because for me God is just an escape for the old. They get nourished by its sprit. So, I say the Hell with that mess of shit! When she went to close her book she felt a sharp pain along her side. She got up to get ready for work when the pain came again until she could not move.

She crawls on the floor reaching to for the phone realizing that something was wrong holding herself up with all of her strengthen. She reaches for the phone and calls the ambulance then remembers to call her boss. Just as she hung up the emergence service was knocking at her door.

At rise: a door open Sheri is lying in a hospital operating room with a doctor and nurse standing over saying.

Doctor: Well, young lady we have to operate soon as possible.

Sheri: Why? What wrong can you just give me some medicine?

Doctor: No! Because you have an Atopic pregency a baby growing in your fallopian tube and if it burst you will bleed to death in twenty minutes. Now, She stays to cry saying no I'm not going to let you cut on me. When the nurse touched her hand saying. Yes, you must it's the only way I'll be with and do you have anyone to call. I said yes and called then gave her the number. After My oldest sister who told me to sign the forms and she had the same procedure. Then the social worker came in replying let's get ready.

Social worker: Hello! Miss Davis, I just need to check over everything to see if all your information is correct.

Sheri: Do I have to as the tears continue to fall having her face to be sad.

Social worker: Yes, my dear I'm afraid so you just relax and signed these forms and let us just pray it will be alright. Right then the doctor came back replying Well, let's get ready we do not want this thing to burst.

Curtain

ACT ONE

Scene: III: Late Evening

At Rise: The sage is filled with smoke simulated using dry ice to give off a cloudy structure. As Sheri is being lifted from her hospital bed she sees them operating on her and is slowly moving upward away until she flowing through massive clouds before landing on an ocean shore. Looking around wondering where she was then suddenly a figure began to appear and she heard the soft music of Mahali Jackson song "Let's walk over Heaven." As she listens the figure got closer and began to talk Welcome to the promise land I'm dreadlock Mike. Sheri was speechless mumbling are you God where are we am I dead? At this point the man was directly in front of her both (center stage). The man was tall and had long braided hair wearing jeans and a long white cloth. He replied that he was not but he would be my guide during our journey and his name was Mike but most people called him Dreadlock.

Sheri: asked how and why did I get here crying saying exactly what state is this and am I dead?

Dreadlock: No, you are not dead yet but, I told you're in the promise land and you are in the state of transposition.

Sheri: What the fuck is all this mess I must be dreaming still crying.

Dreadlock: Hey easy my daughter stops the crying because you are in the state of External Life and you are chosen to go on a journey to help you understand the power of the Almighty.

Sheri: Why they were operating one minute I saw myself rise and landed here on this beautiful beach. Because when she stopped crying and let go of her fear she looked seeing a breath taking place.

ACT: ONE

Scene: III LATE EVENING

Dreadlock replied WHY because you seek my child so God sent me to give you a tour because you are headed for a disruptive path.

Sheri: what do you mean I simply question the mere existence of this thing they call God and religion because of the present state of the world specifically in our country. You see if there was a God why has he allowed so much greed, racism and the rich to control. So, I cannot believe a loving God would have us to suffer in the hand of the elite can't he see how they cheat. This is why it's hard for me to understand all that absolute power stuff you see I was born to suffer.

Dreadlock: Well, that why I'm here to help you over stand the role that God and his religion plays in your life. For you must seek your true purpose or you will be doomed in the state of Hell having to fight your way thought many demons.

Sheri: I do not understand why you can't simply tell me if there is a God then what race and how does he use absolute powers to just bring on storms or distress.

Dreadlock: Our God has many powers this absolute power that you speak of is what we all posse. It a power that we hold within ourselves that resides inside our heart mind, body and soul. You see, Gods powers can be thought as one conscience to refrain them from temptation and obsessive behaviors which steers them away from seeking their purpose. Now, my child come with me and let me take you on a journey that will set your life on its righteous path so you do fall into an unrighteous wrath. Because our streets are not paved with gold but our gates are made of pearl for only the wise pearl can enter the best of humans. For many are created but only the purposeful beings will be granted to live in the promise lands not every women or men will be given the right to this External Life.

Curtain

ACT TWO

Scene I: The next Day

She and the Dreadlock started walking it was breathtaking they entered pastures of green grass and the women were bathing their children in the ocean. The home had beautifully suckled roofing painted in bright colors. As travelled I saw churches that were constructed like big Cathedrals decorated with all typed of gold, brass and sliver. We entered a church and were immediately seated. The people were dressed in bright colors and the preachers were talking about persevering one Soul and helping those who are lost in the darkness. They were looking for volunteers to go assist the unrighteous. After service we went to a restaurant that also was a club. The waitress was smiling giving us a type of menu that was similar to a computer. The Dreadlock explained that this was paradise where no one had to think twice. Making all who came already had fame. Because in heaven no one entered that did not master their purpose on earth first.

Sheri: But it hard to do that on earth because of the unevenness of the wealth. The rich do not want the poor to accomplish their dreams. You see, I was born into a world on fire judging one because of the color of their skin. So how can I make it in world where there is no equality.

Dreadlock: Well my child you forgive because those who chose greed along with hate cannot be granted to enter. There are no big corporations holding our purse string. Nor are there anyone judging by the color of one skin. Look around we have people of every races simply living with honesty and loyalty. Also, we live without any jealousies because all have a share in the profits. That why you must seek your purpose in order to come back because whatever you're doing on earth will surely be instrumental in the decision process.

Sheri looked around and saw the people listening to a concert being preform by several of artist like song in the song by Johnnie Taylor's called Soul Heaven. Suddenly, she began dissenting in downward spiral. NOTE: This is indicated by lowering the stage lights then turning them off and on several times.

CURTAIN

IN Search of my Soul

The Promise Land

ACT TWO

Scene II: AFTERNOON

AT RISE: The stage is set darkly lit and a group of people are outside a gate huddled around a bonfire smoking. Sheri thought one might have been dreadlock and approached while one gave her the smoke. She hit it as gave it back replying where the Hell am I. They all laughed in unison saying yeah haahaha!

One stood up saying loudly "WELCOME TO HELL." She began to see the homes were very dirty old painted in dark colors having no beautiful waters nor landscaping everything looked old and everyone had some type of sickness or body part beginning to change this place looked very wary. A lady in the group told her that this was where the lost Souls landed to continue to seek their purpose. Now, as she began to walked she heard from another women which puzzled her because she shout," you proably have to save someone else soul being given a test before your grant external rest. Sheri did not want to tell her that she did not fully understand. She only knew that she did not want to be there and was willing to do whatever it took for her to get out. Moreover; before she left the group they told her to be very careful of the rapist, murders you name it was down there along with hate, envy and jealousy that ran rapidly through out Hell. As she walked she heard the voice of the children fighting she moved closer to the noise as it got louder. She arrived at a small building outside some students gathering around her hollering at each other when one came in her face. She asked them to help her when one shout fuckin you bitch. Another we are not your personal yellow pages. Then other started pulling on her when the dreadlock appeared they all stopped. He informed her of her task which was to reform the minds of those youths. She told him that she did not understand why. He replied that this will help her understanding of life in general that will give her an unbreakable faith to prevent a most certain fate.

At this time a short intermission:

At rise: the stage is set for a typical classroom with students of various ethnicities. Sheri writes her name on the board. The students are all over the place throwing pencils paper, books and doing anything. Some even were walking on desks others were kissing they did notice her when she shouted, "hello sit yaw asses down! They all stopped as she faced center stage. She turned facing the audience with their desk turned back towards the middle of the stage. (Keep it practical) One student shouted who the fuck you're talking too bitch!

Sheri: Now, that I've got your attention let's get started I will be teaching you basic writing. So, let's begin by introducing ourselves each spoke one student said his name was HATE. She replied that this was too much negative energy and would find another means for him to vent. They began to laugh then as time passed she started reading poems such as "A Hell's Walk" and "The Gambler's Row" along with having heart filled discussions. We talked about drugs and religion we discovered that most did not believe that they had the power inside of them to overcome any obstacle including their temptations. She explained to them how she overcame her by challenging herself to ask the almighty to simply destroy the taste constantly and asking for repentance which made her strong. Because in the world I lived race played a large part of it structure this is why many like I become obsessed with a sauce and controlled by substance. We ended each class with a poem from her or the students who wrote," Through a Child's Eyes." Finally after several days a bond was built which allowed her to not only become their teacher but a friend as they learned to write out their anger they began to love themselves. This gave them a fighting chance to recreate their bond with religion and God. She realized right then that God and religion were one of the same just like peanut butter and jelly you can have one without the other but it will be dry and hard to digest. While she headed for home the group of friends met earlier invited her out for a night on the town.

Curtain

HELL'S WALK

As usual walking keeps us in touch with our souls. But when you walk with Devilish thoughts everyone pays. Having one to walk back and forwards.
Which is harsh on your brain. Causing your sprit to be damaged making
Unwise decisions. Using your eyes to wear a disguise.
Allowing bad ideas of how to live.
So, people must never perform walks that are not of the norms. Which causes Satin to form in your head. But, if you do good deeds this get rid of the
Devils seed that maybe planted deep in their eyes or soul.
For walking is good for your soul that keeps us in touch with our pride.
But a Hell's Walk is very bold and never ever good for your Soul.

THE GAMBLER'S ROW

As a Gambler thinks they can win time and time again but, they are trying to Build their pride. While they constantly making bad decisions believing that
They are only losing the families television.
As their fate is lost life becomes less to a Gambler.

Cause they not only want to gamble but, just play the game never quiting.
Simply loving a life of crap knowing no one will stay in their lap.
Having to become all sick inside. For their world depends on a throw.
Yes, now that's the Gambler's Row.

Through a Child's Eyes

In a child's eyes they do not see race only the kindness that a person holds.
This bind them to their mother's and father's that makes it hard to let go.
Because children are very smart in understanding cold hearted people from the look in their eyes.

The child can see right down to their soul which tell them in their mind what type of person they are dealing with and how to handle them. This is why one should never be to mean to children for they hold the key to simply enable our heart to remain free.

Then they will not grow up with hate falling into a devilish fate which cannot mold only scold. Adults must see that through a child's eyes the world around must be strong for they see truths that will become lost using abuse. Because no matter what you adults say child like souls will lead the way.

ACT TWO

Scene: III

The club was not like in Heaven it had nothing elegant simply bottles and cans the people all looked stuck up and wore dark clothing remembering how nice it was upstairs she began wistfully thinking .After awhile The heavy metal bands and the music of the gangster rappers start giving her a head ace and the flashing dark lights made people less visible. (This should be practical)

At Rise: When the curtain rises the stage is fully darkly lit. The furniture is dirty and old with loud music playing. The customers are gambling fussing and cussing at each other like madmen. The people are dressed in old clothing mostly wearing jeans and tees. (A disheveled attire dark colors) Enters Sheri and the friends she met June and Angela all wearing tight jeans and designers shirts they order drinks then three guys approached asking them to dance. Angela grabbed a guy and ran to the dance floor. When watching she notice that he had a slim built but his eyes were coming out of his head making his forehead to look real big. Once looking around She notice that they all had some of their body parts to start in a phase of deformation. This club was unlike the one that she visited in Heaven having it to be very open and soft music but in Hell down stairs it was pure cut throat. She and June began to dance. (Sheri and June right center stage Angela left) the others were dancing in the middle having several of to be dancing around them seductively. As the music stopped another came she and June moved to the left center stage watching. She asked, Hey are they all this way because if so we are going to have problem up in here, June replied to lower her voice and not say up because down here everyone simply deal with what circumstances that they are faced.

Sheri: what the fuck just like black people! Well we say whatever because what else do we have to lose please who cares.

June: Yeah, now see that attitude is how you got down here in the first place.

June: Yes we may be on the wild side but around these parts we still must seek our purpose and it's difficult because we do not have much time. They saw an open table and ran to it as they sat down they signal to the others then ordered more drinks. Sheri began to talk to Charles who starts telling her that he was there because of his love for that potion. When she asked him what was he talking about he told her that he could not get his drinking under control and suffered a heart attack and other problems. June shouted let's not go there let's just have a good time as she went back on the dancing floor. He continues to talk telling her that he was trying to stop before his body got into the full transformation because he did not want to be banished into the land of the BOBO.

Sheri: BOBO what the hell is that!

Charles: Well you know the Beweavauls.

Sheri: Now what exactly are you saying because I heard that A LOT DOWN HERE.

Charles: Now, legend has it that this is our 1 chance to repent and seek our purpose before our souls gets deeper into the darkness. Then our bodies become part of the soil unless wee sale it to stain. You can think of it like being reincarnated but you always are in the hands of the devil.

Sheri: Is that why it's always dark having no day light.

Charles: pretty much because this is where all the dirty mother fuckers come to rest still in the circle of pain having nothing meaningful in their life but strain. So, they have to fight for everything. They became close sitting talking all night.

Just as they were about to leave Angela was standing center stage among a girl and a guy. The two began fighting over her saying that this was her bitch and he'd better leave her along. When Sheri tried to help Charles pulled her away saying;

ACT TWO

Scene: II

Charles; Now, that's why I hate bitches like your friend.

Sheri; how the hell you say that anything goes here.

Charles: because if a woman chose dick then she should not want to stray.

Sheri: I 'm strictly for victim D but, some women and men want both for that's not my thing. You see my only problem with the whole concept is that it I need victim d after any oral transaction and not that fake shit okay. Along with no seed can be derived from those encounters.

Suddenly, Angela replied that she had a little bit of everything before she was stricter with an illness. Charles let go of Sheri moving over to Angela looking her in the face center stage replying that she need to think about her sexuality more because even homosexuals have to remain innocent and pure to not to weaken their soul.

June came into center stage replying come let's go as the fighting gotten intent. The guy was Tony who was covered with blood as the other woman breast was bit off. Tony had his buddy named Norman to help while shouting that no one owned anyone down there and continued to fight. As the others began to exit Sheri heard a voice saying come (Having the light stage lowered). The stage is darkish coming center stage is a dark skinned women. Sheri said Darlene?

Darlene: yeah it's me your sister,

Sheri: what are you doing here you did not have any real bad obsessions except food and being mean.

Darlene; Yes, that's what I thought too, that not important listen we don't have much time. You see I have over come my demons and I 'm here to tell you that you are head for the land of the Boweavaul.

Sheri: why what have I done I have not harm no one nor been mean.

Darlene; you must continue to seek your purpose before your transformation is completed and you will not be with our mother nor the rest of this family.

Sheri; what do you mean I teach the student and get less pay they treat us like we are nothing down here even on earth they are haters.

Darlene; Hey stop all the complaining you're acting just like me in denial of all my fought remember how I let my weight be my excuse for not seeking my purpose.

Sheri: So what have I done it's hard to find your purpose with all the turmoil.

Darlene; you must fight off all that bad desires because only the individuals who have fought to maintain their reason for living will enter up stairs. And sorry for how I treated you I was not in a good place in my life.

Sheri; so, you mean that you no longer take those pills remember that the darker you are the more one has to struggle.

Darlene; Hey stop all the complaining you're acting just like me in denial of all my fought. Yes even with the prescription drugs I thought just by then coming from a doctor that they were not harmful along with my love for food. But I was wrong. Everything you do that removes one from their blueprint in life that the creator has planned for you will keep you lost in the darkness and in the other world. You do not want to be banished to the BOBO land ok.

Sheri; I heard about all that Bobo stuff is there any truth to that crap.

Darlene; well believe because I did not and paid a heavy cost fighting my way out of this darken where anything goes was the worst thing to happen because it's full of every mean type of humans that are slowly being transformation an insect like creature that's lost its battle with his makers

Sheri; so, you do not chant to the Buddhist faith anymore because you did not believe in God.

Darlene; Yes, but you must over stand that religion and God are like worshipping the Gods. Just as the people long ago did with their different Gods we do that with honoring the different sects of religion okay. So, I found that God and religion was the meat which enabled me to view other people's problems. Now, by finding my God allowed me to heal having me to let go of my hate of everything. Also you must not let the hate and prejudices stop you from you obtaining your purpose. So, stop worrying about all the rich and making lot of money because your purpose is the key to get you back upstairs. Now I must go because I've got thought all this mess and must go to teach music upstairs.

Sheri: music I remember when you use to teach us as she bent down to get her number she was gone. LIGHS LOWERED

Curtain

SHORT INTERMISSION

ACT TWO

Scene: III

At rise: Sheri is in bed with Charles they knew that this was goodbye because He informed her of his personal struggles telling her that she was not the only one who had demons to deal with but men don't tell. So they wanted to hold on to each memory possible. Charles began to rub her face saying :(The stage is lightly lit with typical apartment and bedding furtuniture). The rest of the other rooms are off stage. They both getting dressed sitting on the bed.

Charles: why didn't I meet you years ago things might have turned out different?

Sheri: Well, I realized that love is not only to add spice to one life but it brings a sense of sanity even in this madness. I never thought that it would come especially down under.

Charles: yes say that again because I surely never imagine that loving anyone period. You see, as most men we hold our feeling inside and don't tell as life puts us through all kinds of living Hell.

Sheri: What, we also have many issues it's not only the men.

Charles: Really I thought it all about the size. You know most of you women rate ltd, STD, and bald don't try innocent.

Sheri: yeah maybe when I was young we have a system like little tiny, small tiny and hey both started laughing. Then Charles gather her saying let not let this love we found go. I know that we will be apart because that the way things go down here, but at least we found what was absent.

Sheri: yes that right because after a bad marriage or even a love one become locked in a world of dark rains. Not wanting to feel again and that what this love has taught me. Finding my purpose is only part of the struggle.

Charles: remember that I was love that next time I will not look for happiness in a substance but the love real love of a mate that no bull that's the only way to flow.

Being connected is the key to let go of life's miseries and the trickery as long as one has love they got a chance to hold the line. You see. With me I thought if I lack confidence then I could make it up with fucking,

Sheri: What? How can you get confidence from making love?'

Charles: that's just it confidence is something that gets mixed-up with courage because a man gets yew shay and think his genital are not adequate for the women of their dream.

Sheri: So, is that why most men have to had a lot of women

Charles: I cannot speak for them but for me I did but with you I feel an aching in my bones.

Sheri: for me I feel a passion so deep that it moves me into a world where I longed to go that I thought was long gone. Thinking that a "wife pain" was all that I had to live with. I never knew love like this being loved feels good. I got it mixed-up with lust.

Charles: well don't feel like you're along caused I've loved them then just leave until I was hit with this ton of bricks.

Sheri: but even if we're not every lasting I can be thankful to be removed from the baggage of the past. BECAUSE AS we part you always have a place in this here heart. Both moving as she asked can I sleep inside you tonight.

LET'S SLEEP IN

Come my darling let us feel the heat, and tell me you love me as we lie between the sheets.

Never feeling scared, only anticipating the next move, as we slowly explore a passionate groove.

Then listening to our bodies steam, as we both rise up from a field of dreams.

Take me over and again, for we have passed the point of mere friends.

Wildly we take our bodies on a path, trying hard to not reveal the rejections of the last.

Simply wanting more, but not as a common whore, but what God placed us on earth, for to examine new heights in love making, that's not for the taking.

So close our eyes, and listen to our voices, as we make soft murmuring noises.

Oh, please my darlings do not tease, for we both aim to ease. Let's just lie still for this love must be God's will, for it has enlightened our life. So, my darling you must let me sleep inside you tonight.

ACT TWO

Scene: III

Charles: look her in the eyes saying why certainly with no fear my dear. They stayed together until his untimely departure or the world unknown. But she knew that she would not be sad for very long because that the way love goes. She only could rejoice in knowing that she could love again her heart was no longer tarnished by the storm of his husband nor from the pain of the others. She believes that love and God was much in the same only one is more personal as the other is one claim. Because if one can love then learn to love again that's helps each to achieve that allows them both to release their stress then they been "Twice Blessed"

Twice Blessed

Even though our romance is gone the perils of our love will linger on. For your love was like an addiction a dream fulfilled making my world no longer blue. Coming out of the storms renewed into the norms. With only the memories to keep the warmth of your touch imbedded in our brain that will relieve life's stress. Now one can say love we've been twice blessed...

Curtain

ACT THREE

Scene: I

AT RISE: The stage is set for a typical classroom. At entrance Sheri stops at the door to stay the substitute's prayer to herself then proceeds. The student is sitting quietly talking among themselves and stops as she come center stage.

Sheri: Hello! Class I'd like to thank you for the freedom to teach. Using methods to develop your consciences thoughts in whatever choices you make. Although it was difficult at times you gave an understanding of life that I will hold deep inside because through you I found my true purpose.

So, remember when you're in a storm write it down and give it to the almighty not the greedy preacher or tempting desires. In the circle of life in order to make righteous sacrifice embrace change. She moved closer to the students who were all seated. Let me leave you with a method and a prayer that enables you remove obstacles write your troubles in a form of poetry then give it to God. Because no one's life will be prefect for everyone will have problems if not welt you just might as well not be living. Then she recites "When our Souls are down "and A Substitute's Prayer.

After she read them she asked for any final question before class ended.

Students; in being righteous do we have to live our lives like saint?

Sheri: No! just have a bottom line in your life and over stand what anit.

Another student asked; let's say we buy this Bobo stuff r and seek our purpose how do we know what it will be something that's for them.

When our Souls are Down

Our Souls are down when cruel people set into our hearts and while were down they have no simpathy. It's like the mighty Cheetah when it sick they can not hunt for there food.

That's like the sickness in cruel people whose souls are closed.

Then a sunset upon us brings us to life's full circle causing the cruel people to happily die out. Then one can began to stand on frim ground never allowing creulty to hold

Sheri; you have to understand the signs not being envious nor jealous of other who achieve. Just do not carry hate it blocks the positive energy from flowing directly from GOD.

Another student: Who stood up saying now how can we stay in repentance when there are nothing but murders, rapist robbery you name it anything go down here,

Then another students stood replying yes not to mention how they cheat us in schools teachings only how to pass test just to get souls. They all seem to be in agreement and stood in unison. Still another said fuck all that we will never obtain full repentance because we all are not living in a righteous system from the get go. How can some come down here with riches and another come without even a fucking home.

Sheri: Hey! Now you know those are the obstacles that will prove your worthiness making you strong to fight for your right to seek your purpose. To never leave this place of ill intent with becoming bitter nor none of those riches get one upstairs so just light your own battle because surely as one is born individually. So will they come to the Lord individually judged? No matter what one have to go through if you preserver the almighty will here. Because it's not what a person has been thought that counts but how they came out. Never worry about what you have comparing your accomplishment to others just do your thing Okay!

Curtain

ACT THREE

Scene: II

Sheri left the student feeling sad and she missed the touch of Charles just thinking about their last time together made her think of their adventure downtown and through the valley of pleasure would be hardto fill. So when she got a call from June to meet her at church she agreed. She said well I must practice what I preach and start getting dress for church.

AT RISE: The stage is set for a church with rolls of three. The pulpit center stage facing the audience. As she entered she notice that there was not any crosses in the church. Looking around she also did not see her friend and continue to walk around it was dark and everyone wear dark clothing. The preacher stood at the center stage dressed in a dark suit with a diamond ring on each center finger. As she walked the preacher was promising to give life of riches if they sold their souls. Suddenly her friend June was with Tony waved to her and they found a seat.

Sheri; Well Hello! Nice to see yaw!

Tony: yeah! Same here even if it was a short meet.

June: Well hell it was fun.

Tony: fun that what you call fun fighting with all the drama.

June: yes, and since when did not you like drama

Tony: But not all the time I'm ready for a change.

Sheri: I hear you on that because we don't want to go into the Boweauals.

Sheri: Did you here from Norman?

Tony: Well, you know how it goes either you go up or down but you can't do both.

So, they began on their road to redemption and remained friend until there untimely departure.

Sheri started everyday talking to her students and incorporated in her lesson plans oral discussions about the importance of learning History and poetry. This along with other techquies such as having the student watch movies from past help her to show the students why History was an important part of our culture. Also, they developed a closeness that allowed her to bond with each other that enables her to teach with known conviction because she realized that it was not about monetary gain simply the students. Once the bond was established she could freely teach them whatever she felt they needed to learn about the past. Suddenly, an upward decent began to her raising her out of the darkness and into an awareness that defined her purpose in life. She knew that if she returned to earth that she would be guide by her unbreakable believe in the absolute power of God who maybe many colors and from various of cultures but he resides in us all. Some may call it our consciences or mind but he is the beginning and the end of all life.

So, just as she came to Hell she was taken and she knew that her life had changed in a manner that will keep her on a righteous path with an unbreakable believe in God and people. For now she knows that all humans function under a higher power and we must try to leave our footprint in the sands of a peaceful existence and allowing all that seek the right to at least a home. For as her travels taught her that our blueprints are done from birth and will be revealed to each and every one before we leave this here earth. Once we learn to follow his commands we can also leave these generations footprint in the sands. Retruning to eternal life was wonderful but, just as she came she left with swiftness and never did ever feel the loneliness that she felt. She awoken in the Hospital she began to cry feeling very sad as she looked around she saw that she finally arrived back on earth.

Curtain

ACT THREE

Scene: III

As she awoken from her hospital bed looking around she felt sad and along wanting to return she began to cry when the doors open it was a tall white lady wearing all white clothing. She replied welcome back you were out for a long time. I said how long was I out Two week we were worried about you glad to see that you are alright how do you feel, Okay I guess. She started fixing the curtains saying we must get you up and walking. I was crying she turned around looking me straight in the face having her blue eyes to look directly in my face saying now listen to me carefully, I nowhere you been and why. He sent me to help you readjust to earth. So, please do not be upset because you were sent back it simply not your time yet. Why I said I do not want to come back. She replied that not up to you nor me to say just remember if you take your own life you will still not return and you will become trapped between Heaven and Hell into a wall of darkness for that will be a sin against the most high. You must follow the commandments to be granted external life. Understanding that one's personality controls one attitude whereas creativity controls one thought together they will guide your beliefs. Now, let me help you <**>a bath and I'll give you a nice massage. Sheri still was crying as the nurse continued to hold her telling her that she must be strong and faithful.

Twenty years later she became a substitute teacher and ran her class just as she did in Hell the only difference is that the students are not all deformed only bad. She then began to search for her a home and got it paid for so when all you critics say that I do not have the credentials to write on the homeless saturation. I just tell them I got mine from the most high. He along with myself believe that In the words of Thomas Paine whom wrote so eloquently in the 18th century that this nation will never be a nation of law-abiding citizen as long as we all are inherently doomed from birth

In concluding Let stop narrowing the housing market to exclude the oppress putting them through so much paper work and work together to give anyone that seek the right to live in a decent home without this government always wanting to 'Break the Soul of a Folks...

The story begins in winter of 1980 in Lansing Michigan Where Sheri Davis is going on a journey that puts her to find her meaning of God. She thought that this thing called religion was surly Made up because of the poverty she felt along with her race. While going through a major operation she encounters a world that set her entire life on it path to preserve through obstacles in Heaven and when she's suddenly descended to Hell. Which enable her to form her only personal views of what role love, religion and God places in her life? So, in these difficult times she'll no longer worry about the elite or the one percent he sees how they cheat. They too will have to meet because one thing is for certain death is everyone's' FINAL CURTAIN. Now, I hoped you like this play and it made one think because we live-in a world that's on the blink. Please let's wake up we've all suffered from CSS and CHS far too long. Come rise in all nations to choose our leader as if we'll seeking our soul mate. Choose those who can remain loyal to its people with Honesty, Integrity, and Equality. Those whom can bring us all into the future with no strings attached. YES, THEIR SELF ESSTEEN WAS HELD DOWN. Being sold as cattle but somehow still fought the battle. And pray one day at a time that tomorrow would be forgiving then kind because never ever will there be a time again that the slavery of a people will settle in. You see, Equality is not only for the betterment for the Africans Americans but it reflects the hopes of all citizens by every means,

Malcolm X

CHS – Can't Here Shit
CSS – Can't See Shit

The course along with the journey taught her to OVERSTAND that as we all try to leave our footprints in the sands remember our life's blueprint is in the God's hands. Leaders stop "BREAKING THE SOUL'S OF A FOLKS" WHILE" IN SEARCH OFTHEIR SOULS," AND THEY WILL NOT OCCUPY SIMPLY GIVE US A FAIRSHARE OF THE PIE.

The End

I 'AM FREE

By
Shelia Cunney

From the depths of our passion to the hurt of the past
I 'am Free.
From using the Lords name in vain which causes one to reframe
Not to go insane.
I 'am Free.
From the sorrows of the last while learning to open up to another
I 'am Free.
From having the Lord to remove all our burdens because he knows when we are hurting
I 'am Free.
From replacing the storms of our past to be removed with no strings Attached,
I 'am Free.
Oh, yes, yes I'am Free to simply live, love, and enjoy to just be free from the pain and shame placing no one to blame I 'am Free to go peaceably.

Afterthought

O come by here our Lord of Lords and King of King, we seek glory before entering in the most beautiful land that's not known to most men.

You see, one must realize that you can only help them through someone else because you're far too busy to come down as yourself.

So please let the readers of this book not fall upon still minds of the leaders.

But is taken world wide and cause the Homeless to rise above their present condition.

In a strong but gentle manner to firmly climb the ladder out of there Homeless state. Away from shelters of lost Hope and reap through the world's harvest of wonderful beauties, and let the leaders minds tingle with truth and righteousness for the people without homes to pass on to their offspring. For they must over stand the needs of the Common man so that we all are afforded the same opportunities and can be treated in a humane way as they are rising out of their Homeless condition.

Let this be through-out shelters in this nation in these days that surly test our strength in human brotherhood to not make a mockery nor snare upon nor be given food in sheltering places that are not fit for human consumption but given the proper chores that enables them to earn wages that truly allow them to purchase a home to pass on. Thus our children should never be in shelter such as Miami, Ft. Lauderdale, Detriot and Houston that do not allow them to grow mentally, physically and socially.

For they can grow to make serious contributions to the future of America.

Therefore; presidents of shelter like Mr. Richard McMillan of the star of hope in Houston missionary shelters and various of others like in Los Angeles to stop the repeated revolving door enacted programs of meaningful intent stop the treatment of workers who feel that the Homeless is hopeless and must be treated without any dignity and they can not do or have any of the pleasures in their lives while being Homeless like to even watch the news or if you do not want them to eat a proper diet let them bring non parish even they have rights while Homeless. Finally never allow your policies and programs and your present procedure that enable the workers to be breaking the Souls of a Folk.

For even the meek will have to answer to THEE.

Out of the faith of the fathers
A haunting of this world has caused faces to be dim
In sprit lacking a beauty that belongs
There filling shelter of lost hope into a hurled of despair
Why don't we care their left alone to go to heaven with?
Not even obtaining a home.
Where alone they must stand accounting for all their
Earthly demands not even being given a fair means to advance.
May the Homeless of all races find peace within THEE?
For God will provide those a place if they don't lose their Grace.

Sources

William Edward Burghardt Du Bois; "The Souls of Black Folk" 1868–1903 reprinted, 1994, Dover Publishers Inc. New York.

Thomas Paine: "Common Sense," 1997 Dover Publishers Inc. New York

Norman Vincent Peale: "The Power Of Positive Thinking" 1992 Fawcett Books, New York

Happer, Hard-court, "Our World Today People Places and Issues," 2003 McGraw-Hill Inc. New York

Holt, Rinehart, and Winston: "American Nation in the Modern Era," 2003 Time Inc. New York

Dr. Jesse Glassor: Breaking the Chains of Poverty," 1990 Vantage Press, Houston Texas American 10 commandments 1997 Angel Gifts, Inc. Fairfield, Iowa

Props List

Table of Contents

Act One – Early Morning
Scene I
Podium
Classroom Desk
Chalkboard
Pictures of Religious Phosphors
Scene: II – All Standard Equipment- Afternoon
Hospital Bed –Standard
Clothing (Social Worker, Nurse, Doctor) Standard Uniforms
Scene: II Standard Apartment Bedding Late Evening
Fog Machine and/or Dry ice To Stimulate Cloudiness
On Stage: In Heaven; Beautiful Surroundings
(Trees, Flowers, Clean Landscaping Etc.)
On Stage: In Hell; Simulated By Diming Lights
(Red Lights on Dirty Structures)

Act Two – Later That Night
Scene: I Standard bar Equipment
On Stage: In Hell (Tables, Bar, Nothing On the Bar & Tables)
Hell: Loud music (Guns & Roses & Gangster Rap)
No Glasses Bottles Only, Dirty Surroundings
Scene: II the Next Day
Classroom Standard Equipment
Apartment: Sofa, Lamps, End tables, Coffee Table, (Center Stage)
Bedroom: Bed Bedding 2x Lamps & Nightstands
Kitchen & Bathrooms: Locate off Stage

Act Two – Early Morning
Scene: III
Church – Standard Equipment
Center Stage- Pulpit, Chair

(Red Lighting with Green, Gold, Black, Purple Surroundings)
Characters Clothing Attire; Dark & Wintry

Act Three – Afternoon
Scene: I
Character Attire; Wintry
Scene: II Evening
Hospital Standard Equipment
Characters Attire Wintry
Hospital Workers Clothing Standard Wintry
Scene: III
Hospital Bedding Standard
Nurse Attire Standard

In Search of My Soul

Music List

ACT One:
Scene I: LeAndrea Johnson, "Jesus"
Scene II: Mahalia Jackson, "Walking Over Heaven"
Scene III: Johnny Taylor, "Soul Heaven"

ACT Two:
Scene I: Gangster Rap and/or Gun & Roses "ANY"
Scene II: Kemowens, "If It's Love,"
Scene III: Beyonc'e, "One plus One"/

ACT Three:
Scene I: Estelle, "Thank-you"/
Scene II: Mary J. Bilge, "You need someone to Love"
Scene III: Rance Allen & Paul Porter, "I Will Trust In You"

In Search Of My Soul

Property List

Acts: One, Two, Three
Classroom Consist Of Desks, Blackboard, Chairs, Center Sage Teacher Pulpit Students Desk Center Sage Roll of (3)
Apartment Consist Of Living Room, Center Stage Living Room- Sofa, End Table, Lamps, Coffee Table
Locate Downstairs, Left Dinning Area-Right Stage Kitchen & Bathroom off Stage
Bedroom Consists of Bed with Bedding End tables (Upstairs) Lamps, Candles, Rugs on Floors All Other Shelves Have Books, and Tables Are Bear with Only Lamps. The Main Entrance to Apartment Is Located Center Stage. When The Door Is Open Living Area Downstairs and Bedroom Is Upstairs Over Living room. Center Stage Upstairs When Bedroom Door Is Open Is Shown A Bed Etc.
Heaven Consists of Misty Beautiful Paintings with Bright Lighting Colors of Landscaping's Very Clean Picture of Various Messengers Dropped All over Center Stage. (Keep This Practical).
Hell- Darkly Lit Red Lighting Surrounding Center Stage. Pictures of Satan & Devilish Worshippers Dark Red Velvet Curtains &Carpet Red.
Club-Heaven Big Dance Floor Brightly Lit Beautiful Tables & Chairs With Napkins On Top; Computers Pictures of Various Religious Figures Dropped In Silver, Gold, and Copper & Brass Surroundings The Walls. Statues Are Placed At Entrances, Characters Attire Nice & Neat Wintry Clothes
Club—Hell Dirty Surroundings Small Bar with Nothing But Loud Rude People. Red Lighting Throughout The Stage, Everyone Fussing In A Madness Type Of Atmosphere Characters Clothing Is Tight, Short, For Females. Males Wear Baggie, Sloppy Attire.
Church- Customary Heaven Consists Of Crucifix Of (Gold & Silver Polished To Perfection. Diamonds, Rubies, & Other Jewels on Door Handles & Doors. On Walls Hand Paintings Hang off All Them, Pictures of Religious God Depicted on Them. The Book Of The Dead Was Dropped Over The Walls. Hell Church Was Small Looking Like A Storefront With Red Lighting And

Dropped With Demon Skeletons, Pulpit Center Stage. Character Clothing Dark & Wintry. Paintings of Skeletons on Walls. Horns of Gold on Walls & Devil Worshipers.
Upstairs In Heaven It Was Peaceful With Hindu, Buddhist, Jewish, Christian, & Islamic Statues And Values & Teachings Cover The Stage.